# CHECKMATE

# CHECKMATE

DAN PELED

# CHECKMATE

*iUniverse books may be ordered through booksellers or by contacting:*

*iUniverse*
*1663 Liberty Drive*
*Bloomington, IN 47403*
*www.iuniverse.com*
*1-800-Authors (1-800-288-4677)*

*ISBN: 978-1-5320-7690-9 (sc)*
*ISBN: 978-1-5320-7691-6 (e)*

*Print information available on the last page.*

*iUniverse rev. date: 06/11/2019*

# PROLOGUE

The man with a few minutes to live ran on the hard sand of Black's Beach under a sun now passing its zenith. The sea gulls resting at the water's edge, disturbed by his passing, screamed in anger and cleared a path for him. The man shaded his eyes with his hand as he glanced up at the magnificent cliffs towering above him to the east.

The cliffs gleaming in the afternoon sun were etched with the shadow of a winding path snaking its way down to the beach. The massive wall of rock provided security from prying eyes for the nude bathers lolling or playing on the sand and made the runner feel strong and secure. He felt the packed wet sand under his bare feet, breathed the salty air deep into his lungs, and picked up speed. He was soon trotting at nearly six miles per hour and sweat was running down his spine.

Roger drove his Land Rover down the serpentine road leading toward the beach and parked it behind large rocks, out of view. He turned off the engine and alighted the vehicle with a long tan canvas bag. The sun arched westward beyond the cliffs and shadows fell inside the clearing where the Land Rover was parked. He removed a pair of field glasses from the glove compartment and swung the leather strap over his head, resting the binoculars on his chest.

Roger climbed inside the crevasse of boulders, heading slowly toward the cliff's edge overlooking the water. He was soon breathing hard. He held onto the long canvas bag, balancing his climb against the sharp rocks protruding from the narrow opening. When Roger reached the top of the fissure, he saw the ocean and a breathtaking line of white water moving toward the shore.

He laid the canvas bag on the edge of the cliff and adjusted the field glasses to his eyes. A runner was in full view, framed inside the binoculars sights. The runner's pace increased, his long muscular legs seeming to catapult his lean body forward.

Roger scanned the runner's path along the water's edge. Two women were walking toward the runner, and beyond, a group of nudes were immersed in a volleyball game.

Hmmm, he thought to himself, as a woman lifted the volleyball and served it into her opponent's court. Her breasts collided as she lunged forward, following the ball.

Roger switched his binoculars back to the runner and saw the runner's gaze shift toward the woman also. She was crouched in a defensive position, waiting for the volleyball's return to her court, unaware of either his or the runner's roving eyes.

Roger removed the rifle from the canvas bag and began assembling the scope. Leaning against the cliff, he raised the rifle onto his shoulder, focusing the scope on the runner's lean torso, then his head. Satisfied that it was the man known as 'The Water Boy,' he rested the rifle against the rock and continued to follow the runner's path. He took his cell phone out of a pocket in his windbreaker and punched in a number.

A deep voice greeted his ear.

"Eric here."

"It's me, Roger. Everything looks good at my end. He's moving south."

"Wait for him to turn around."

"Agreed. This has to be a no-fail." Roger raised the field glasses toward the runner.

"It will be," Eric assured him, signing off.

Roger leaned against the cliff. The first time he'd ever heard of The Water Boy was in the Caspian Sea right before an oil rig exploded and a red bowl of fire knocked him a dozen feet into the air; he'd awakened later in clean, cool hospital sheets to find a pretty nurse bent over him, changing his blood-soaked bandages.

The terrorists escaped, but shreds of the bomb and a sleek fiberglass speed-boat were later found floating in the oil-soaked waters of the Caspian. He carried a souvenir from the incident—an ugly scar on his thigh, throbbing now, just thinking about it.

A lot had happened since. Roger raised the field glasses, again tracking The Water Boy's path along the beach, as memories came flooding back.

# CHAPTER 1

The party was in progress when Roger arrived. Wet snow was falling outside and the air was freezing. A damp harsh wind blowing in from the bay followed Roger into the house. He took off his coat and shook off the snow.

A few people stood by the fireplace watching as a man stoked the flames and laid on a fresh log. A woman with black wavy hair to her shoulders stood nearby.

The man tending the fire looked up. "Hello, Mark," Roger said to him. The man straightened and came towards him. "Roger, you made it despite the weather."

Roger hugged him. "We've got to talk ASAP," he said quietly.

Mark nodded.

"Some interesting people here," Roger said, looking toward the woman at the fireplace.

"Leah Golan, my student. You might know her father Aaron."

"The Aaron Golan? Head of Israel's special operation division?"

"Yes, and consultant to the Defense Ministry. Let me introduce you."

The two moved towards her. "Leah," Mark said, "Roger Shaw, an old friend of mine."

Roger extended his hand, feeling the velvet touch of her fingers as her green eyes met his. He noticed a dimple in her right cheek.

The doorbell rang and a woman wrapped in a sheepskin coat, hat

1

and scarf entered and looked over at them. "Hello," Mark said, going towards her.

"What brings you to Boston?" Leah asked, surprising Roger, who was busy looking at the newcomer.

"The cold weather." They both laughed. "So you study under Mark Lindsey?"

"Yes. He is absolutely the best."

"So you're a scientist?"

"I'm working on it."

From behind Leah, Roger saw Mark Lindsey and the woman who'd just come in moving toward them. What had emerged from all the cold-weather wrapping was a young, tall blond with a lean athletic figure not quite hidden under a heavy black sweater. She lit a cigarette and Roger noticed long lashes and a straight Roman nose. Her soft hazel eyes, framed by curving eyebrows were directed at him with curiosity.

"Do you know her?" Roger asked Leah, as they watched the young woman make her way across the room.

"She's my roommate."

"Hi," the woman said to Leah and hugged her. Then she turned to Roger. "Linda Ashcroft, another of Professor Lindsey's students."

"Roger Shaw," he said, holding out his hand. She took it, smiling warmly. Whereas Leah's touch had been soft, Linda's was electrifying.

A young man with a tray of drinks approached them. Roger took two glasses of wine from the tray and offered them to the women.

"So you teach at Harvard too?" Linda asked him.

"Oh, no, I'm no scholar."

"What are you then?"

"I'm a humble lad from Idaho." Both women laughed.

"You don't strike me as humble," Linda said, smiling.

"You don't strike me as a Boston native."

"I'm not. I was born in New York, though my family roots are in Colorado. My grandfather was one of the founders of Vail Village."

"Well, my granddaddy was a logger who cleared the biggest ski run in Sun Valley," he answered and smiled his perfect-teeth smile.

Linda grinned back. "You got me there, your granddaddy wins."

"I have skied Vail, though. In my early life, when I was in college."

"When you weren't roaming the world, you mean," Mark said, coming up behind him.

Roger smiled at him. "I admit it. I follow the path of the wanderlust." He moved closer to the fireplace to make room for his friend. They went back a long way, to the summer they'd met in France while hitchhiking around Europe, two nineteen-year-olds seeing the world.

Mark held up his glass. "Here's to new and old friendships." The others raised their glasses to him.

"So what does a guy from Idaho with wanderlust do for a living?" Linda asked.

"Excuse us, ladies," Mark said. "Roger, will you help me bring in some firewood?"

"Sure," he said and followed him out to the snowy backyard.

"We have to talk. I have urgent news," Roger said, as Mark pulled a tarp off a cord of wood.

"Shoot," Mark said, filling Roger's arms with a stack of fireplace logs.

Just then, the back door opened and Leah leaned out. "Mark," you have a phone call."

"Coming," he said and grabbed an armful of wood himself.

"Tomorrow, early," Roger said.

"You name it," Mark answered.

# CHAPTER 2

An icy wind blew off the Charles River as Mark and Roger walked together along its snow-covered bank, bundled in down jackets to ward off the bitter cold. Mark raised his collar against a sudden gust of wind. "So what's on your mind?"

"The Iranians are shopping for nuclear and biological weapons. We need your help, Mark." He paused, looking at the frozen river.

"The Iraqis have been at it for a long time, way before the Gulf War. Now the North Koreans are in the market too, so are the Chinese. But the big spender is Gregory Pluchenko, the Russian Mafia chief. He controls an enormous amount of money and goods."

Mark listened without comment, as they walked briskly through the crusted snow-pack, their gloved hands deep into their coat pockets.

"But there's more to it. Much more," Roger continued. We have information that Pluchenko sent out feelers to none other than Kamal Ibn-Sultan, the alQueda terrorist. My people are telling me that Ibn-Sultan might be hanging out in Afghanistan."

Roger looked toward the river again. "The man is definitely a big problem, a conniving son-of-a-bitch and a survivor."

"So where does all this leave me?" Mark inquired.

Roger picked up some of the fresh snow from along the bank, made a snowball, and pitched it at him. It hit his chest and Roger darted away laughing.

Mark followed suit, and soon icy snowballs and taunts flew between the two. After the battle subsided, they brushed snow from their coats and hair and Roger became serious again. The river-bank was deserted, except for a few sea gulls looking for an elusive prey. "The director asked me to tell you that we need your advice at the agency."

"On biological weapons?"

"Yes. We have to nail Ibn-Sultan. We believe that he is the official stand-in for Bin Laden. Whether Bin-Laden is dead or not, Ibn-Sultan is carrying the torch. We have information that something huge is going down, probably with Pluchenko's help."

"Aren't you telling me too much?"

Roger smiled, flashing his whitel teeth. "We trust you. I trust you. You're my friend, remember?"

Mark nodded.

"You did some biological weapons research on your own, Mark. We think you have vital information that the agency needs to supplement what they have."

Mark looked at him, puzzled. "You don't mean the project that Linda Ashcroft is working on, do you?"

"That's precisely what I mean. I want her on my team as soon as she graduates," Roger said.

"You sound determined."

"I am."

"I have no problem with that, but she's looking forward to an academic career with the university. I'm afraid you will have to ask her yourself."

"I already have" Roger told him, surprising his friend with the speed of his reply.

"When did you two have time to discuss all this?"

"She gave me a ride to my hotel last night."

Mark laughed. "You're incorrigible. I bet you gave her that old steelhead fishing on the Henry's Fork of the Snake routine."

Roger smiled at him. "Hey, I presented a genuine offer. Of course,

I pointed out how many of you Hah-ved faculty have bellies sliding towards your knees. Not yours of course, not yet."

"Not ever, my friend. So, what was her answer?"

"I'll know tonight. I invited her to dinner."

Mark nodded. They stopped and looked toward the frozen river in silence. Finally, they turned back toward Mark's house, facing into the icy wind coming off the bay.

"But I'm certain her answer will be yes," Roger said.

"Why is that?"

"She said she loves trout."

# CHAPTER 3

S andra sat at her piano facing a large picture window overlooking the East River in her plush Manhattan apartment. She was playing her favorite Beethoven piano concerto, Molto Allegro, and the music reverberated against the window as she watched a lone merchant ship plow its way through the ice floes in the river below.

A log crackled in the fireplace, and the warmth of it carried toward the piano, on this afternoon at home alone. Although she was beautiful, intelligent, talented, and that men were drawn to her, Sandra was single. She had known a few men in her life. The first was Chris Long.

Chris had been her science teacher at the university, a handsome man with a square jaw and dark eyes—the married father of two young girls. Once they had gotten involved, Sandra would feel his eyes boring into her during class, as though he were recalling their most recent stolen hours of pleasure.

Sandra met his wife and children at an awkward party at his Cape Cod home on the occasion of his youngest daughter's birthday. He'd invited several of his favorite students, Sandra among them, just four months after their secret love affair had begun. He'd smiled and hugged his wife Daphne in front of her, but his eyes remained on Sandra the whole time.

During the party, he had taken her on a tour of the place and then led her to the barn, where he kept his horse. Riding was a hobby Chris loved dearly. There among the hay bales, accompanied by a restless pounding of hooves, he caressed her and kissed her. They became aroused and he entered her, raising her against the stable wall. She heard Daphne outside, calling her husband back to the party. "Chris, we're lighting the candles," she yelled from the back yard.

Chris climaxed with a groan and Sandra felt his warm seed inside her. They broke away and quickly straightened their clothes. She followed him outside, where Daphne stood looking at them. Though she smiled, her worried eyes searched Sandra's face. Sandra smiled at her too, to assure her of an innocent visit to the stable. The three of them walked back toward the main house, then Chris said lamely, "I showed Sandra the horse; she loves him."

Daphne looked at him with a strange look, but did not speak again until they reached the house. Sandra knew she suspected them, but Sandra was so in love she felt no remorse.

Several months later Sandra missed her period; she was carrying Chris' baby. When she told him, he made it clear that it was her problem and left her to wrestle alone with whether to have the baby or get an abortion.

She didn't feel she could turn to her widowed father for help. The former marine officer was not only straight-laced and ramrod in attitude, he was a slave to his work. He had transferred his love of duty to the corporation he headed, an insurance company in Hartford—his newest front. It was a theater of beaches to storm and mutinies to crush that left no time for his only daughter.

Except for telling Chris, she carried her secret alone and found an abortion clinic in New York City. Chris did not offer to help her with the expensive procedure and Sandra finally went to her grandmother in Manhattan. Sophia, her mother's mother, was the only one to come through for her, with warmth, shelter, financial help—and advice.

"You must be careful, my dear, that you do not become involved with men like your father," Sophia warned her. "It is a woman's greatest challenge —to not find her father in every man she meets, unless of course he is kind, gentle, caring. Yours is not. Beware, dear."

It was a boy, the doctor told her after the procedure, a healthy boy who could have been hers.

Then there was Tony. Anthony Savino was a rising young executive in the small pharmaceutical company she joined in Boston, after finishing her masters' degree at the university.

He was in the corridor, his arms full of files when she emerged from the office where one of his superiors had just offered her a job as research associate. The position came with a nice office, a secretary and a research budget for developing advanced formulas for baby food.

Tony had held her gaze as she walked toward him. He was tall, clean cut and carried himself gracefully, his wide shoulders all too apparent through his tight white laboratory coat.

"I'm Sandra," she said, extending her hand. Then realizing he couldn't possibly shake it with all those files, she'd laughed shyly.

"Tony Savino. You have a great smile, but your eyes intrigue me the most."

She had not known how to respond to this straightforward comment, but she liked it.

Over the next eighteen months, she worked hard. Her career took off shortly before their wedding when she moved to a job at a bio-chemical concern as senior researcher at twice her former salary. The firm, a competitor of the company Tony still worked for, specialized in advanced research on the human cell.

Tony, unlike her, had been unable to advance with or surpass his associates and was upset by it. She tried to reassure him, for it didn't matter to her in the least that he still held the same position. For by now, she was in love with him. Tony Savino knew how to make her happy. When he caressed her body, instinctively knowing how to make love to her, first softly, then savagely, he took her to a place she had never known.

What did matter to her, however, was that she suspected him of using drugs. Whether they were over-the-counter or something else, she didn't know.

At first, she thought it was the alcohol. But on the eve of their wedding, though he had been drinking, he became so animated, so frantic and so unaware of her personally, so just plain scary, that she had wondered what he'd been doing before joining her. He had come to her door late and pushed her toward the bedroom, his eyes glassy and unfocused. "What's wrong?" she'd cried. "Nothing," he said as he stripped off the bed covers and threw them across the room. He yanked her onto the bed roughly and essentially, took her.

She still recalled the incoherent sound he'd made, an animal's cry, before falling into a fitful sleep where he called out someone else's name.

The next day, despite this huge flag of warning, she'd married him anyway.

They were happy for a while, or were they? She had not wanted children, although Tony liked the idea. She was deeply involved in her work and would come home exhausted after a busy day at the office to find Tony, always waiting for her with a glass of wine.

As the months and years went by, she realized that perhaps it was not really what she wanted, a nice town house in Boston and a husband who took mind-altering drugs with wine chasers while waiting for her to come home.

One night, on a return from a business trip to New York, Sandra found the house empty. A note on the kitchen table told her that Tony had gone to meet his bowling buddies. She put her things away and went to take a shower. She'd just turned off the water when the phone rang. She grabbed a towel and ran to answer it. It was her friend Joan.

"Sandra, I'm so glad you're home."

"What's up?" she asked. Joan sounded like she might be crying.

"Can we meet for dinner?"

"Tonight?" Sandra was tired and wanted to go to bed with a book.

"I need to talk."

"Is anything the matter?"

"Please, can you meet me at Legal sea food in an hour?"

She agreed and put on jeans and a sweater, checked her phone messages, glanced at her mail. She grabbed a jacket and hurried to her car. It had been a long day and she was in the middle of a tough negotiation. Her company was bidding to acquire a small, profitable competitor in New York.

She found a parking spot a couple of blocks away from the restaurant, locked the car and hurried down the street, trying to guess what was on Joannie's mind. On the block near Legal's, she noticed a very familiar leather jacket and unmistakable head of coarse blond hair. She stopped, staring in amazement. Indeed, it was Tony, not ten feet away, kissing some young girl outside a shop. The area was crowded with students and no one cared but her. To everyone else coming and going that night, it was just another couple kissing.

Infidelity on top of drugs was too much. That moment, realizing that it was all over with him, Sandra went home, packed some things and left. She never did find out what had been troubling Joan that night.

After a long, stormy divorce proceedings during which Tony hid his own assets and sued for hers, Sandra took off some much needed time from work and flew to the Cayman Islands. She spent her time lazily, catching up on reading, sunbathing and swimming.

The first time she saw Ray was at the pool. She first noticed his dark head, darting through the water, back and forth, one lap after another, again and again. She returned to her reading, until suddenly, he hoisted himself out of the pool with an effortless movement of tan, strong arms. His body was lean and graceful and she couldn't help stare at him. He grabbed a towel and shook his full head of thick, black curls and disappeared around the corner.

The next day, she was surprised when he came from the bar carrying icy drinks and sat down in the lounge chair beside her. "For the sad, beautiful woman who stares at half-naked men," he said, handing her one of the two drinks.

She was embarrassed. "Really, I don't usually stare at men," she said. "You're just such a strong swimmer, I was impressed."

"I am honored," he replied. He downed his drink, some kind of tropical juice, abruptly nodded to her and left. That alone was enough to intrigue her, and the rest of the next few days she kept one eye open for the good-looking foreigner with the accent. He reminded her of Omar Sharif. She suspected that he lifted weights maybe, and probably did a lot of jogging.

He finally approached her again, this time in the dining room at the resort where she was staying. "The sad lady who is always reading," he said.

"You mean when she's not staring?"

He laughed. "Yes, when she's not staring."

She held out her hand. "I'm Sandra. Please, won't you join me?" she asked, though she had already finished eating.

"Ray," he said, kissing her hand. "I would rather take you for a boat ride. The water is like glass right now."

He was right. The next thing she knew, the two of them were skimming across the very calm waters of the Caribbean, in a small power-boat, going too fast to hold a conversation. She merely held on for dear life, without taking her eyes off him, as he steered the vulnerable little craft, bouncing its way across the bay.

"Tell me about yourself," she said later, glad to be back on shore and strolling beside the gentle surf instead of riding on top of it.

"Not much to tell," he said. "I was raised in Israel, studied languages, moved to America as a young man, enlisted in the army there, became an importer-exporter when I got out of the army, and now sell expensive goods to rich people all over the world. And you?"

"I work at a pharmaceutical company in New York."

"Good," he said. "I visit New York often."

That night she made love to him. In contrast to Tony, he was gentle and caring. And because she had liked Tony's rough, combative style, she was surprised how easily Ray satisfied her, emotionally as well as physically. It was true intimacy, she guessed.

# CHAPTER 4

The man known as The Water Boy laughed. His laughter reverberated through the canyon and broke into a thousand syllables against the rocky walls. Tall mountains loomed in the distance, snow still capping their peaks.

The camel driver, Suleiman was telling him a joke about the former President of the United States and the man held his belly, his laughter startling the camels that were urinating on the rocky sand of the canyon.

"A man of many talent, this American president, with his cigar and all. But I think his own people in the Senate did him in; not the people of the land, but those lawmakers," Suleiman said, piquing the other man's interest.

"Who told you all that?" the man inquired of the camel driver. The driver wore a black Keffiyah, and his eyes peered through a slit in the dark fabric.

Suleiman laughed and raised his head skyward. "It's old news, discussed on CNN long before he left office. It's a small world and getting smaller because of all of the satellites and instant TV coverage."

"And I took you for a simple man," the stranger said.

"I am a simple man." The camel driver smiled at him, then busied himself with the animals, checking the load on each of the beasts to assure that the precious cargo they carried was secure. Then he turned to the stranger.

"I have a message from Kamal Ibn-Sultan for The Water Boy."

"The Water Boy?"

"That's what he said," the camel driver told him.

The camels became restless, and Suleiman motioned toward the beasts, as if to say that the journey must continue. "Kamal told me to ask for him. He meant you, of course."

The stranger nodded, cracking a smile at him. "Word travels fast, I guess," he said, watching the camels get to their knees at the sound of Suleiman's shouting, despite their huge loads. He put his hand on Suleiman's shoulder. "What did Kamal say?"

"He told me to tell you that he'll wait for you near the Khyber Pass for two days. That it is important you be there."

Suleiman led the camels out of the canyon in the direction of the far away mountain pass, holding the lead camel's rope to guide the small caravan. The stranger walked alongside him.

"Tell no one about my meeting with Kamal," the stranger warned him, waving his finger in front of the camel driver's face.

Suleiman's face turned red. He was visibly insulted.

The stranger tried to appease him. "I am sorry. I am sure that you are a loyal man, but as you know, danger looms everywhere. The Americans are after Kamal's ass and I must not be caught in the fray. I have much work ahead of me."

Suleiman looked at him suspiciously. "I understand. Still, if Kamal trusts me, you should too. I talk to no one, not even to my wife about such things. I gave my solemn word to Kamal, our Rais. I worship the ground he treads. I too want to unite Muslims of the world in a Jihad against the infidels."

"I trust you Suleiman and I apologize," the man said softly.

Suleiman noticed the stranger's dark, penetrating eyes, which showed no emotion, though his lips smiled.

"Can we make it to the pass in two days?"

"If we ride non-stop, and with Allah's help," Suleiman advised him.

"Let's start then."

Suleiman nodded, shouting at the two lead camels, forcing them to kneel. He mounted the lead camel and the other man followed behind and got on the second one. After another command from Suleiman, the camels rose slowly to full height, lifting their passengers.

Then the caravan began moving slowly toward the Khyber Pass.

———

Kamal rose from his mattress at dawn. He got out a folded rug and walked outside the cave. Sheaths of pink were rising behind the mountains in the east, as dark shadows began fading in advance of the sun moving down the slopes of the mountains.

He spread the rug on the earth near the entrance to the cave, fell to his knees, and bowed his head toward the east and Mecca. He touched his forehead repeatedly to the rug as he prayed in silence.

By now, sun had melted the light frost and he stood up and folded the rug. Once back inside the cave, a phone rang. He took a cellular phone from his robe pocket and pressed the button. "Aywah," he said.

"Ya Rais," a man's voice spoke, "The Water Boy has come."

Within minutes the camel driver had bade his camels kneel and he and the other man dismounted and started to unload the supplies. Kamal approached them, signaling to one of his men to help. "Please, not here. In the vehicle," he said to the camel driver and led the way.

Once they had all the cargo on the ground, Kamal barked orders to one of his men. "Let Suleiman rest and eat before he leaves. And pay him the usual. My guest and I will be in my office."

Kamal and the stranger went inside the cave to an area flooded by fluorescent light, in a comfortable room with thick Persian rugs and deep chairs. "It's good to see you again," Kamal said. "Please, sit down."

A man brought in a tray of coffee and Kamal was silent until he left. "Now, have you a solution to my problem?"

"I do. We can buy the goods and then transfer them into the United States using a Russian submarine that can travel undetected in American waters. I know someone who can arrange for both the product and the sub."

"I like this idea if it is foolproof."

"Foolproof, but expensive. I can arrange for you to see the sub."

"Of course. Who is your connection?"

"Gregory Pluchenko."

"The Russian mobster? He is broker for both the sub and the chemicals?"

"Yes."

"Can we trust him?"

"You have a long arm, Ya Reis. This man does not dare either to cross you or to pass up such a profitable deal. And as a new contender for power in his own country, he has many enemies already."

"Good, maybe you should get to know a few of them."

"Indeed, I will."

"Make the arrangements."

"Right away."

Kamal opened a box near his chair. "I have a new phone for you. Destroy your old one. This is a state-of-the-art instrument. You can call worldwide with the same clarity as talking to someone at home. It is indeed amazing."

He handed one of the several that filled the box to his guest. "I have phones for whoever you pick for your team also. But I caution you, use them only if it is a real emergency. And then talk in code. The American satellite is not without ears—or eyes. Tonight, we will change locations by moonlight, in case the satellites watch my truck as well."

Kamal rang a bell nearby. "But now let's have breakfast and discuss the best men for our project."

# CHAPTER 5

General Golan, whose capers as a tank division commander during the Yom Kippur War had become legendary, opened a file on his desk. He was now in charge of managing counter-espionage and anti-terrorism at the Defense Ministry.

The general rose, looking intently at the two men sitting in front of him, then began pacing in front of a large map of the Middle East and Asia. Abruptly, he turned to the tall man whose dark hair had begun graying prematurely.

"Ben," he said to him, "Did you get this information from Leah?"

Ben nodded and got to his feet for a better look at the map.

The man still seated, Oded Eitan wore a military uniform with the insignia of general, army intelligence.

"When did you meet her?" the intelligence officer asked.

"Yesterday, in New York before my departure."

General Golan had not seen his daughter Leah for quite some time, not since her college graduation in June, and he missed her terribly. She was his only child and he had become very close to her after his wife passed away from cancer the previous year. He raised his eyes anxiously to Ben.

"What did she have to say?"

"First of all, she sends her love."

"And?" Golan asked impatiently.

"She told me of the American plan. My men have confirmed it through their own connections."

"What is this plan?" General Eitan inquired.

"The Americans are now suspecting that Kamal Ibn-Sultan has something in the works. He met recently with a man known as The Water Boy."

"How did Leah get this information?" Golan asked.

Ben sighed. He would have to tell him, sooner or later. He turned to his old mentor and looked him squarely in the eyes. The general waited, his face alert with curiosity.

"Leah is involved with her old professor at Harvard, the one you met at her graduation. Mark Lindsey. She adores him. Don't be mad at her. It's her first true love."

General Golan began pacing in front of the map, and then turned to Ben. "How can I be mad at my own daughter? She's a grown woman, is she not?"

Ben nodded, looking at General Eitan, who shrugged, though a smirk on his face revealed something other than indifference.

"Yes, she's a mature woman and will be fine. I hope you don't have any problem with the fact that she is now working in my group," Ben added.

"Would it matter?" Golan asked. "Of course, I prefer that she go work at some research company, but as you say, she is a mature woman."

"Life's full of twists, as you well know. It was a surprise to me too when she decided to assist us, instead. But she'll be doing research, she will certainly not be in the field."

The General nodded, acknowledging the fact that his daughter was the mistress of her own destiny. "Anyway," he said, returning to his desk and the open file.

He leafed through it and removed something from a side envelope attached. It was a photo of a young man in Egyptian paratrooper commando fatigues, wearing bars signifying his rank of major. He was smiling at something in the distance. The tip of one of Egypt's ancient pyramids was prominent in the background.

"Take a good look."

"Who is it?" Ben asked.

"The Water Boy. Here's what we know about him: He's tight with Kamal Ibn-Sultan. He's been in the military, maybe an ex-commando, probably with the Afghan rebels in their fight against the Soviets. That's likely where he met Ibn-Sultan. He was also deeply involved with the Muslim Brotherhood movement banned in Egypt. And we're certain he was tied in with the people who killed Anwar Sadat. Recently, he's been seen in Muslim neighborhoods with known terrorist organizers."

"Why is he called The Water Boy?" Ben asked.

"Well, I doubt it's true, but popular myth has it that as a young child he dutifully packed water to his father's oxen in heavy tin cans on his head—thus the title given to him by his brothers that he's still known by." Golan paused "We know all this, but we don't know who he is."

"How can that be?" General Eitan asked.

"Perhaps Ibn-Sultan has purposely kept him in the shadows."

"Interesting," Ben said, skimming the pages. He passed it back and General Golan retrieved Rashid's photo, attached it to the file, and handed it on to General Eitan.

"A phantom scoundrel," exclaimed General Eitan, looking up from the file.

Golan nodded. "So, let's hear what you've got," he said to Ben.

Ben began detailing the data he'd received of Kamal Ibn-Sultan's whereabouts.

# CHAPTER 6

"Here's something that's going to rattle your cage," CIA Deputy Director John Devine told Roger one Monday morning by phone.

"Rattle away."

"I don't know if you still sleep with Al-Sharif's file under your pillow, but the man's reaching out to us."

"What!"

"That's right. In fact, he asked some of his old CIA contacts who the best person for him to meet with would be. Your name came up and he's requested you."

"I definitely want this gig."

"Figured that. So, here's the deal. He wants to meet in Istanbul. At the Ciragan Palace, on the Bosporous."

Roger knew the area. The palace sat high above the shoreline—and in the right light, its ornate facade reflected in the swift waters of the Bosporus Strait below. "So, what do you think he's up to this time?"

"No idea. He merely hinted to his contacts that he had vital information and wanted to convey it to the right man at the agency."

"And that would be me."

"Knock yourself out" Devine said, and hung up.

Roger certainly intended to, for he had made a serious study of Rashid Al-Sharif. He not only did not appreciate ex-CIA who played it both ways, he thought this particular one had become a terrorist. He had compiled research, kept meticulous notes, and generally followed his movements for years. That is, when he surfaced, for Al-Sharif was apt to disappear for months, even years at a time.

According to his research, Rashid Al-Sharif had been born to a poor family of farmers in the Nile Valley where they had eked out a living. An army recruiter had come to the area when Rashid was barely seventeen years old and inspired Rashid to join. His superiors soon discovered his talent for languages and sent him to a special training school for gifted soldiers.

After several years Rashid emerged an educated young man able to speak, in addition to his native Arabic, English, French and Hebrew. The army then sent him to boot camp, and from there after serving as a corporal in a paratroop unit, to officer training. The young lieutenant later returned to his unit to command a platoon and eventually rose to the rank of major. He had become a polished career officer.

His life changed drastically while training with American troops in the Sinai Desert prior to the Gulf War. Rashid befriended an American commander and confided to him that he would like to join the CIA. The American officer made the contact for him and Rashid was catapulted from a structured life as an army officer into the dangerous and unpredictable world of espionage.

Although he worked hard to please his CIA superiors, he was soon branded as an untrustworthy operative. Ties were abruptly severed when officials suspected that he was operating as a double agent for this reason: on a visit to Italy, Rashid contacted a Hezbollah terrorist group based near Milano and convinced the group that he worked for the CIA. After the agency got wind of this duplicity and cut the contact, Rashid disappeared.

A year later he surfaced at the American Embassy in Cairo where he managed to obtain a visa to the United States from an unsuspecting embassy official. The CIA had issued warnings to immigration officials that Al-Sharif might try to come to the United States, but none were heeded and Rashid succeeded in entering the country.

After several years of constant contact with various government agencies, Al-Sharif enlisted in the American army and joined one of its elite commando units, the Delta Force. Although not directly involved in the unit's operation, Rashid soon became the company's supply sergeant and later trained as a paratrooper, achieving a high-performance rating.

Then the man disappeared.

Where has he been? Roger wondered. And why was he suddenly in their face? Roger didn't really like the idea of meeting with him—he preferred being the shadow at his back.

Roger decided to throw him off a bit by having Linda make the contact instead. Of course, he would be there in the background, studying the scene. Why not Linda? He thought. She had been working full time for the agency the past six months under Roger's watchful eye. She had just enough experience to handle a simple meeting, but not enough so that she would be known by Al-Sharif or anyone trailing him.

Moreover, Linda had an uncanny intuition, a sense for getting the bigger picture at a glance. She had become his main source of information on the growing biological warfare mania involving Iraq, Iran, and lesser rogue states like Libya. And Roger had a hunch that Al-Sharif was deep into that very thing. In fact, he and Linda, with his friend Mark's help, had already begun the formidable task of tracking a smuggler's trail of certain equipment and resources, no doubt being moved and gathered in order to produce biological weapons.

# CHAPTER 7

The time and place for the meeting with Rashid Al-Sharif was soon set in stone, and Roger and Linda got on the first of several flights that would take them halfway around the world. They traveled separately on different airlines, two days apart.

Linda flew British Airways to Gatwick where she caught a connection to Istanbul. It was her first flight since the 9/11 disaster and she guessed that this was the case for many of the other travelers aboard. There was a quietness, a respectful introspection going on among the passengers that she could feel. One could not help but contemplate the horrific sequence of events that must have taken place in the skies on that morning.

It had been those events on that fateful day that had really persuaded her to change career directions. She wanted to do her part to ensure that lawlessness and extreme fanaticism did not prevail on earth.

Roger was the first to arrive and he re-acquainted himself with the city and the palace where they would meet. When Linda got there, she took a room at a different hotel, in another section of the old city, miles from him.

The day of the meeting, as agreed, Linda reached the palace first.

She spent an hour or more among the buyers and sellers spread across the grounds then slowly approached the rendezvous place under a hot, bright noonday sun. She wore a cotton skirt, a T-shirt, sun hat, and sandals and carried a basket she had just bought from a merchant. She looked the typical tourist.

Roger followed her through the throngs of people milling around the marketplace, appearing to check out the various goods for sale himself. He wore a pair of old jeans, a short-sleeved shirt and sunglasses. A Turkish merchant was busy arranging his wares at the stand, where Linda and Rashid were supposed to meet.

Rashid was already there. He too wore dark sunglasses and old jeans. He looked toward the palace once, Roger noticed, perhaps expecting a third person to join him.

Then Linda approached and Roger moved in closer, trying to pick up the conversation. He was unable to catch what Linda said, as though her microphone had quit working. But she had obviously asked Rashid for a light, because Rashid spoke briefly to the merchant who produced a match or lighter. Rashid lit Linda's cigarette and handed back whatever it was to the merchant. The two then wandered slowly among noisy vendors hawking their wares.

Roger followed, adjusting his own wire, and suddenly he could hear them clearly.

"I was not expecting a young, attractive woman," Rashid said.

"The man you were supposed to meet could not make it, so I came instead," Linda explained. Rashid was eyeing her with suspicion, she noticed, and watched as she drew on the cigarette.

"Not a healthy habit."

Linda smiled. "I know. But meeting someone like you, in an exotic settings for reasons unexplained is stressful."

Rashid's dark eyes softened at that and he smiled. Her unexpected candor had broken the ice. This was her first real assignment and she was nervous. She had caught a glimpse of Roger's face twice already, peeking through the crowds of tourists that swarmed the merchant booths.

Linda decided to take the initiative. "So, you have a message that needs delivering?"

"Yes, of course," he answered with a slight hesitation, calmly surveying the surroundings. He took a manila envelope from his inside left pocket and handed it to her.

"As you no doubt know, I used to work for the agency in Egypt while serving in the army. Tell your people that I want to come back."

"I will make certain that my people know that, Mr. Al-Sharif."

"Please, call me Rashid."

"Rashid," she repeated.

"Could I buy you a cup of coffee or lunch perhaps? I know a wonderful restaurant down the road near the Bosporus."

Suddenly, Linda saw two men approaching rapidly. Then Roger materialized out of nowhere, motioning to her to leave quickly.

"Next time. I have to . . ." Her sentence was interrupted by one of those men, now at Rashid's side. "May I see your ID papers?" he said to Rashid. The man spoke in English with a Turkish accent. A palace security man, Linda guessed, as she moved to distance herself from the scene.

"Not so fast, young lady," the man's companion said, as he closed in on her left. She noticed that Roger had disappeared in the crowded palace yard. "Your papers, please."

"Of course." Linda took out her American passport and handed it to the man.

"Just as I suspected, American," the man said. "What are you doing in Turkey?"

"May I ask who you are?" Linda asked. The man wore a thick, black mustache that curled upward, and his quick, black eyes darted from her passport to his companion, who was still interrogating Rashid.

He ignored her question. "Your name?"

"Linda Ashcroft."

He leafed through the passport to confirm, then compared her to her photo. He returned the passport. "It is a tight situation. We are looking for two escapees, from one of our prisons. Kurdish rebels, both armed."

"Do I look like a Kurdish rebel?" she asked with annoyance.

"Is it your intention to be rude?" He said, his tone ominous.

"No," she said. "I am afraid I have had a hectic day."

The man talking to Rashid lifted a concerned face from Rashid's passport, eyeing Linda. "What's the problem, Yakim?" he said, glaring at her.

"Nothing," the man called Yakim told him. "Leave now," he said to her. "Those escapees may well be close by, for all we know," he added, as though threatening to stick them on her.

"Right," Linda answered, eager to get the hell out of there. She moved as calmly as she could toward the palace exit. When she turned her head to look for Rashid, she saw two elderly tourists standing in the spot where Rashid and the Turkish security men had just been. She hurried through the crowd. When she spotted Roger again, her breathing returned to normal.

The next morning, on the airplane home, Linda found a local newspaper left on her seat. She picked it up and was startled to see pictures of the two security men who had stopped her and Rashid Al-Sharif the day before. A one-word headline stood out in bold above the photos.

"What does this word mean?" she asked the cabin attendant when he came by.

"Murdered," he said, leaning over her shoulder.

Had someone put the newspaper there on purpose or was it a coincidence? This job was making her paranoid.

# CHAPTER 8

John Devine sat on the sofa talking on his cellphone while Roger waited for him to finish the call.

Devine, a burly man in his early fifties rose from the sofa and walked to the large window behind his desk. "You could have brought him in, you were so close to him."

"There were too many tourists and he was armed. I wanted to give Linda her first taste of danger in the field, not get her killed. Anyway, he will be more useful to us if he doesn't think he's wanted. Besides, we haven't connected him to anything definite yet."

"Okay, what have you got?" Devine's pipe had gone out and he bent over a metal waste can and tapped the pipe against its rim to dislodge the ashes.

"He's on the run and wants us to bring him home," Roger said, taking out a manila envelope from his canvas bag. He handed it to Devine who opened it and extracted a photo of a tall bearded man, his head covered with a Keffiyah headgear. He was holding a Kalishnikov, pointing it toward tall mountain peaks covered with snow.

"A nice shot," Devine said. "Kamal Ibn-Sultan is actually a handsome man. This looks like it was taken in Afghanistan."

He turned to Roger for his opinion and Roger shrugged. "It could be Yosemite Park for all I know, John. I asked the boys at the lab to identify it on the satellite." Roger knew Devine from way back and always called him by his first name, sometimes surprising other senior officials with this direct address.

"So, this is all your man gave Linda, a picture of Ibn-Sultan?"

"He's telling us he has information about the man that he either wants to sell us—or trade for a safe exit somewhere."

"To escape what?"

"I think he's gotten in too deep with Ibn-Sultan."

"Isn't that his intention? Ibn-Sultan has endless resources of money and power, and his loyal associates do well."

"Granted. On the other hand, Ibn-Sultan turns on his own, easily. He can find an unfaithful man, no matter where he hides. Rashid knows this, but is still a freelancer at heart."

"So, do you think those men who stopped him and Linda were Ibn-Sultan's men and Rashid killed them?"

"Maybe. Or maybe they were Kurdish rebels. Maybe they were tailing Rashid and Ibn-Sultan's men killed them." Roger got up and looked out the window. "Then there's his personal life to puzzle."

Devine's eyes narrowed with curiosity.

"He has a lover in New York. An executive in a pharmaceutical corporation."

"So? The man is entitled to a piece of ass, isn't he?"

"It's more than a piece of ass. The man is either in love or about to make a major score, maybe an independent one. I don't think it's a coincidence that her firm specializes in bio-and chemical research."

"So, you're telling me that Rashid is looking to acquire bio-chemicals for Ibn-Sultan?"

"Why not? Rashid is devious and his past record speaks for itself. But he might be walking a tightrope nowadays. Maybe he's trying to appease Ibn-Sultan, but wants out of an impossible situation. Thus, an escape route, a disappearance through our agency. A plastic surgery would do him miracles, don't you think?"

Roger paused, watching rain clouds rolling in from the east. He turned from the window back to Devine. "I think he has a bank account in the Cayman Islands, full of payoffs he got from Ibn-Sultan for various favors."

"Do you trust this Rashid Al-Sharif?"

"None whatsoever. The Israelis talk about some secret operative well connected to Ibn-Sultan. They call him The Water Boy. I think Rashid is that man. And I think biological warfare is the next theater of war."

"I agree. These people are nuts. This so-called holy war is no way near over no matter how many operatives we've picked up, or terrorist camps we've destroyed. One way or another, we have to take Ibn-Sultan out."

Roger nodded and rubbed his thigh unconsciously.

"That old leg acting up?" Divine asked, referring to the injury Roger had received in the oil-rig explosion in the Caspian Sea years earlier.

"It's better, except in cold, damp climates. Then it throbs."

"I'll remember that and send you to the Sinai or maybe Afghanistan." They laughed momentarily then became serious again. "So now what?" Devine asked. "Wait for another contact?"

"Yes. Meanwhile, I'm on his tail. I think if he really is The Water Boy, he will lead us to Ibn-Sultan."

"I still can't imagine a major player like that wanting to bail."

"Hey, half the world is looking for terrorists and they will be found. I don't think Al-Sharif is the dedicated crazy Muslim extremist Ibn-Sultan is."

"The picture is certainly clouded," Devine said. He poured two glasses of water from a carafe on his credenza and handed one to Roger. Then he sat down at his desk, referring to his notes.

"Here's what we got on merchants of biological warfare: Viktor Shalyapin, presently a secret state security officer in charge of chemical and biological weapons in Russia and former director of the Verdat Laboratories, manufacturers of deadly viruses for weapons in the Soviet Union. Another one is Gregory Pluchenko, Russian Mafia head, a mover and shaker of nuclear and biological weapons on the international black market. Then there's Reza Deghani, an Iranian counter-intelligence officer and expert in biological warfare.

"Also, we know that Ibn-Sultan made two recent trips to Cuba—as guest of Raul Castro; and he met with someone near the Khyber Pass that the Israelis call The Water Boy—someone you think is Rashid Al-Sharif.

"Shortly after, Al-Sharif contacts the agency, meets with Linda Ashcroft in Istanbul, and gives her Ibn-Sultan's picture; next, the two men Linda sees him with last have their throats cut after their meeting. Also, Rashid has an American lover who works for a company that makes drugs in New York. And you suspect he wants protection from the agency because he's up to some freelancing on the side that Ibn-Sultan might not approve of. Or he simply knows he's in over his head. Did I miss anything?"

"Nope. I'm also looking into the woman Rashid is involved with."

"Good." Devine handed him his notes. "Here, take these for your famous file."

# CHAPTER 9

"That was nice," Sandra Savino said, as she propped her head with one hand, and touched Ray's black curls with the other. They were sprawled on the king-sized bed in the master bedroom suite in the luxurious Cayman resort. "Very, very nice. Funny, who'd have thought?"

"Who'd have thought what?" Ray asked in a deep, groggy voice. He was falling asleep between Sandra's breasts and it felt good. Like a small child held close to his mother's heart.

Sandra smiled, her long fingers deep into his thick curls. "'Funny' is the wrong word. Amazing, that's it. It's always amazing to me, even after all this time, what a turn-on your gentleness is. I never knew that kind of sweetness before you."

"Too many cowboys?" he teased.

"Not too many," she said, slapping him playfully. "Two. Only two cowboys."

Ray opened one eye and kissed her nipple.

"If you continue that, I will attack you. So, please, don't stop, it feels too good, it's like . . ."

The phone at their bedside rang, interrupting her. "Yes?" she said into the receiver.

"Sorry, Sandra, this is Bob. I hate to bother you on vacation but there was a guy around here today asking a lot of questions. And since you're in charge of research, I told him to talk to you."

"What guy?"

"From the CIA."

"The CIA! Are you kidding? What questions?"

"His main concern was whether anybody had approached anyone here, trying to purchase equipment or materials connected with biological research."

"Of course not. But a Russian company presented an offer on a joint venture with us. The immune system, flu vaccines, stuff like that. There's a report in my files with my recommendation. I sent a copy to the Board of Directors. What's he looking for? Industrial espionage?"

"I don't know. Maybe they're worried about terrorism."

"My god, I hope not. But of course, it's a crazy world of late."

"Yeah, unfortunately. You don't happen to recall the name of the person who approached you?"

"No, but it's in the file there."

"So, what was your recommendation?"

"That we not do any joint ventures at this time, though at some point I envision a team of scientists from all over the world working together on certain problems."

"Okay. You better cut your trip short and get back here. The guy wants to talk to you."

"What's going on?" Ray asked her when she got off the phone.

"That was my boss. Someone from the CIA wants to talk to me."

"I heard you say some Russian company approached you."

"Yes, but it seemed harmless enough. Certainly, didn't raise any red flags that suggested terrorism."

"So, this is about terrorism?"

"That's what my boss thinks. You know, Ray, I just don't get it. What's happened in the world to make people so disenfranchised, so maniacal that they would commit suicide just to kill innocent people."

"I think people—nations—have become too polarized. Great is

the distance between the fatted calf and the grain of rice. When people have nothing to lose, when hope is gone, they become desperate. Look at the history of the world."

"Goodness, I'm glad we had pilaf for dinner instead of veal cutlets."

He laughed.

"Though you laugh, I think this makes you very sad."

"Yes," he said. "So many people on earth in pain. And no end in sight."

# CHAPTER 10

"So, you think this woman's selling out?" Mark Lindsey asked Roger, as they got out of the cab in front of the biochemical giant, Laguna Industries.

"I don't know. That's why I wanted you to join me. Her reputation is shiny, maybe too shiny. You'll be able to cut through the bullshit."

"I don't know. Yours gets me every time."

Roger grinned and opened the large glass door for him.

"Roger Shaw for Ms. Savino," Roger said to the man at the reception desk who looked at a directory, put in a call, and repeated Roger's words. "She'll be right down," he told them.

Within minutes, Sandra Savino appeared from the elevator. She held the door for them and introduced herself. Then the three got on. "I didn't mean to keep you waiting but I was in the lab," she said, which explained the white coat over her expensive looking suit. When the elevator stopped, she led them down a hallway to a sunny corner office with a view of midtown skyscrapers, most prominent, the Chrysler building. She took off the lab coat and motioned them to take a seat. And instead of sitting at her desk, she drew up a chair in front of them. A nice touch, Roger thought.

"So, you're the Mark Lindsey from the Harvard team," she said, smiling at Mark. "I know your work. You published a paper in the Harvard Review. 'The New Biology,' I believe it was called."

"Yes," he said, obviously pleased.

Next, she smiled at Roger. "Now, what has brought both a distinguished scientist and a CIA man to my door?"

The two men couldn't help laughing. "We're an unlikely pair, no doubt about it," Mark said. "Actually, we're old friends. Close friends."

"How can I help you?"

Feeling completely disarmed, Roger began.

"Miss Savino, we know that someone contacted you from Verdat Industries about working with them on a project."

She got up and went to an oak filing cabinet near her desk and took out a slim file. She glanced through it briefly.

"Viktor Shalyapin, but I don't see the name Verdat here." She handed the file to Roger.

"He's not really with any company that we know of at the present, Ms. Savino. That's what worries us. He's a secret state security officer in charge of chemical and biological weapons in Russia. And the Verdat Laboratories, which he once headed, were manufacturers of deadly viruses for weapons in the Soviet Union."

"Ooh," Sandra Savino said. "Scientists against life."

"Yes, and unfortunately, there are more out there. You've heard of Ibn-Sultan, haven't you?"

"Yes, he's one of the chief king-pins in the Bin Laden network, is he not?"

"Yes, a person known to have met with Shalyapin."

"Your research and ours at Harvard are running almost parallel," Mark said. "We're in the same position—at the risk of someone using our findings, as you say, against life."

"But what would these people hope to gain from us? We don't make weapons. Our research looks for the cure. In fact, since the recent anthrax threat, we've been working around the clock on a vaccine."

Mark shook his head. "They're betting that there's someone who will sell out some way, contaminate the findings, or maybe they just want to corner the market. Think of the money to be made if you have the vaccine and own all the stock. Then you not only can terrorize the world, you can finance it on the sales of vaccine."

"So, here's what we want from you," Roger said. "We want you to be aware of anyone approaching you or anyone else doing research here, suspicious or not." He handed her a card. "And let us know immediately."

The three of them got up. "Increase your security too. These are dangerous people."

They both shook her hand and headed for the door. Roger turned to her. "May I ask what you filed that Shalyapin thing under?"

"Pardon?"

"You know, what category in your filing system?"

"Industry contacts," she said. "There are lots of those."

He nodded and closed her door.

"Why did you ask that?" Mark asked as soon as they were alone in the elevator.

"I don't know. Sometimes, people give away things they don't mean to when caught off guard. They hesitate, tying to think of what they think you want to hear or they blurt out the truth and then wiggle around it."

"You expected her to file it under "R" for Rashid's friend, or to not have had a file at all?"

"Something like-that. But this woman's hard to figure."

"Hmmm, she did do that pardon, gimme-a-minute-to-think thing."

"Or, maybe, just a what-did-you-say? Things?"

"How come you didn't mention Rashid Al-Sharif?"

"I don't know. I think I'm better off just keeping track of who she hangs out with, without making it apparent."

"So, you've bugged her phone."

"Not yet."

"That's so tacky."

"It's terrorism here, Mark. What happened downtown on 9/11, now that was tacky and a whole lot more."

"Okay, you be the CIA dude and I'll go back to Boston and look for a cure for evil."

"A deal. After lunch?"

"Definitely after. This is on you, right?"

# CHAPTER 11

When Rashid Al-Sharif and Kamal Ibn-Sultan arrived in Odessa, the Iranian Reza Deghani was waiting. Reza was of medium height, wore a goatee and rimless glasses that accentuated his dark fierce eyes. His thick hair was peppered with streaks of gray and a scar on his cheek ran from his ear lobe to his mouth. Rashid knew it was an old wound that Reza had gotten fighting against Iraqi forces during the long battle prior to the Gulf War.

"Aren't these subs built in St. Petersburg?" Rashid asked their host.

Reza laughed. "Yes, they are, but for some customers, the showroom is here. More privacy for discrete tastes."

Reza led them to an old military jeep for the ride to the submarine base where they were joined by the Russian Mafia chief, Gregory Pluchenko. This man had a full head of dirty-blond hair, a Slavic face, cold blue eyes, and large strong hands. Rashid suddenly felt distaste. These were men who had no other purpose in life but to accumulate money and power.

A third man who was neither introduced nor familiar to them did all the talking. He explained that the new kilo class type 636 submarines were just now being completed. They walked along the sea wall adjacent to the port of merchant ships and old military carriers.

"One of them is almost ready for her sea trial," he advised the group in thickly accented English. "Two of the type 636 subs were sold to

38

the Chinese navy and are patrolling the Straits of Taiwan. The type 636 was designed for anti-submarine, anti-surface ship warfare. It was built not just to protect coastal installations and sea-lanes, but also for reconnaissance patrols and missions."

The group stood aside while a crewman let down a gangplank. The group moved forward and Pluchenko and Reza waited on the wharf for them while they toured with the expert on kilo submarines.

"It's considered to be one of the quietest diesel submarines in the world," the man told them. Ibn-Sultan didn't speak, but nodded his approval. "It has a range of detection four times the capability of any other sub in the world, which means it can strike or flee long before the enemy knows it is even in the vicinity."

"Hmmm," Ibn-Sultan said and looked over at Rashid.

The man continued. "It consists of six watertight compartments, separated by transverse bulkheads. This design—and the submarine's reserve buoyancy—greatly increases the kilo's chances of surviving a puncture. It has a sea endurance of forty-five days, and a range of 12,000 kilometers when snorkeling at seven knots, and 645 kilometers when submerged at three knots. It's armed to the teeth with torpedoes and mines."

"A floating fortress," Rashid said, pretending not to notice that someone on shore was looking through binoculars in their direction. "Can you take us back to the city now?"

"Why, yes, of course," the man said.

"Quickly?"

"Yes, how about by water?" the man said, pointing over the side to the marina. "But don't you like our submarine?"

"We do," Rashid said. "But we have an emergency."

"Okay," the man said, "Let's go."

The three climbed down a rope ladder on the side of the sub facing the sea and got into a small craft. The man untied the rope holding it close to the sub and started the motor. When they had gotten to the other side of the port, the man maneuvered the boat to a dock, where several sail boats and other power-boats were tied.

"What should I tell Pluchenko?" the man asked.

"Tell him that we'll get back to him," Ibn-Sultan said, speaking at last. "And that, as the Americans say, you definitely know your stuff."

"What is your name?" Rashid asked.

"Yevgeny Katuzov," the man said.

"Ah, Vice Admiral Katuzov," Ibn-Sultan said. "Former Russian fleet commander."

Katuzov bowed slightly. "At your service."

# CHAPTER 12

The attack was swift this early Tuesday morning. A laundry van pulled up and parked by the side entrance to the embassy, just as staff began arriving. Then all hell broke loose as missiles slammed into the guardhouse and main embassy building. The shoulder-fired missiles exploded almost simultaneously with the one in the van. A deafening sound and red flames shot up from a hole where the collapsed roof of the building once stood, leaving bodies of the dead and wounded strewn around the complex. Nothing remained of the guardhouse at the embassy entrance, nor of the four marines—two inside, two outside. Then, the driver of the van exploded with the compounds of Semtex and C-6 inside it. The other perpetrators of the deed had escaped.

The wail of a siren was the only sound after the explosion and it came from the rear of the building where a fifth marine guard, his face and body laced with shrapnel fragments, had set the siren before dying.

John Devine received the call twenty minutes later. He was at his desk, mulling over news that the Iranian Reza Deghani had been seen with Ibn-Sultan and Al-Sharif at the former Soviet Union submarine base in Odessa, now part of the Ukraine. There a Russian fleet commander, Vice Admiral Yevgeny Katuzov had showed the terrorists around. Gregory Pluchenko, the Russian mobster, had been there too.

'What the hell are they up to now'? He wondered as he picked up the phone. "Devine here," he said in his usual, curt voice.

"John, this is Bernie McBride at the State Department."

"Bernie, what's up?"

"A terrible thing. Our embassy in Ankara was bombed twenty minutes ago."

"What happened?"

"It took a hit from what appears to be a missile, or missiles. Also, a van exploded near the side entrance and it looks like it caused most of the damage. We have twenty-five dead and at least forty wounded, some of them in critical condition. The ambassador was lucky. He arrived late. The FBI's on the way."

"Who's there now?"

"A company of marines, a Turkish security officer, and some local officials. I'll keep you posted."

The line went dead.

# CHAPTER 13

The accordion player paused and switched to an old sentimental melody and the crowd began to sing along. As he increased the volume, people stood up and moved to the music. The musician lifted his eyes from his instrument and watched a newcomer enter the tavern and go toward the back. In seconds, as the melody's tempo reached a high pitch, some of the people began dancing on top of the long tables, despite the vodka bottles, glasses, and ashtrays they had to maneuver around.

"Kalin, kakalyn, kamalin, kamaya . . ." they sang, swaying with the music. The newcomer paused to take in the excited crowd then looked back at the entrance, as if to ascertain that no one had followed him in. Satisfied, he continued toward the back of the tavern towards another man, Reza Deghani, sitting at a small table against a window with his back to the noisy crowd. He was drinking black coffee, though a full bottle of vodka and glasses were in front of him.

The accordion player took a break and Reza Deghani turned to the newcomer. He rose and extended his hand. "Rashid, I am glad you came."

Rashid shook the Iranian's hand. "Reza," he said, "A good choice this tavern."

"How is your friend doing? I hear the Americans have a hefty price on his head after that embassy thing."

"He remains safe despite the bounty," Rashid replied. "He sends his regards. Sorry our meeting at Odessa ended so abruptly."

Deghani motioned for Rashid to sit and then to a waiter who came immediately. He waited until the waiter had taken the order and left them. "What do you think of the product?"

"Very impressed. And we're still interested in the other. We need both, soon," Rashid said.

"How soon?"

"In a few weeks, if you can do it."

"I might be able to arrange it. Actually, I am waiting for Pluchenko now. He has some information that you would like," Deghani said, smiling.

The waiter arrived carrying a tray loaded with two bowls of Borscht, a plate of cold, cooked potatoes, and a pot of hot tea. After the waiter left, they tasted the soup, and Rashid smacked his lips. "I like this borscht. It's the real McCoy."

"Ah, American slang. But no wonder after all those years in the States," Deghani said.

The noise of the crowd increased again as the accordionist played another popular song. The crowd began dancing, laughing, and singing loudly. Only when the song ended did the two men try to talk.

"I hear that you have a woman friend who's a pharmaceutical executive in New York," Deghani said.

Rashid looked at him coldly. "You hear too much."

Deghani grinned. "Word travels fast in the select circle of people dealing in the lines I carry."

"My friend has nothing to do with what I am doing," Rashid protested.

"No one is saying that she is associated with your adventures. Relax. You are tense. Perhaps, you would like a bit of this excellent vodka?"

"You should know better. I am a devout Muslim. I never touch that stuff," Rashid said angrily, his intensity matching Deghani's.

"Sorry if I have offended you. Anyway, this friend of yours might have information I am interested in, and I am not alone, let me assure you." Deghani stroked his goatee and peered over his rimless glasses toward the door. "Ah, here he comes," he said, getting up to hug the big Slav who soon stood before them.

Pluchenko turned to Rashid. "Nice to see you again."

Rashid rose also and extended a hand to him. "A pleasure."

"How is your friend doing? I hear that he runs with the wind from the American's wrath. Evidently his god watches over him," Pluchenko said, revealing a gold tooth.

"Yes, he leads a charmed life," Rashid agreed.

Deghani pointed to the table and Pluchenko joined them and waved to a waiter who hurried over. "I must recommend the borscht," Deghani said.

Pluchenko nodded and spoke to the waiter in rapid Russian. Deghani poured Vodka into glasses and handed one of them to Pluchenko, who took out a pack of Camel cigarettes from his pocket. He lit one and offered the pack to the others who shook their heads. "So, are we going to do some business today?"

"We might. I was just trying to persuade Rashid to introduce me to his American friend, the scientist," Reza Deghani said.

"If I am not mistaken, you're talking about the same woman who refused to meet with my associate, Viktor," the Russian said. "Viktor Shalyapin."

Rashid looked at him and held his gaze. "As I told Reza, my friend has nothing to do with why we are here."

"Her company is doing some secret research for the Pentagon. We want this information badly," Deghani said.

"Find another contact. Several companies are doing the same research."

"I don't understand," Pluchenko said.

"You don't need to understand. But I suggest that you will be the next people to have a prize on your head, if you pursue anyone working for the Pentagon." Rashid got up. "If our business is contingent on my bringing my friend to the table, I withdraw it."

"Wait," Pluchenko said. "Please, sit down."

Rashid hesitated, then sat down.

"On your visit to Odessa you indicated interest in our sub? Do you want it?" Though Gregory Pluchenko smiled, his eyes were icy.

"Maybe," Rashid said. "Do you have this same sub in St. Petersburg?"

"Not at the moment. This is the only one ready to go. You know, we brought it to Odessa especially for you."

Rashid frowned.

"But if it matters, we can transport it back to St. Petersburg."

"Very well."

"We discussed some details, but not money or this change in location," Pluchenko said. "Can you afford it?"

"We have no problem paying you," Rashid answered. "I can order an electronic transfer to any account you choose."

"Where is all this money coming from?" Pluchenko asked.

"You will have to raise that question directly with Kamal," Rashid replied.

"He is good for the money," Deghani assured the Russian Mafia chief.

"A lot of palms will have to be greased," Pluchenko said. "My services do not come cheap."

Deghani held his hands together in a conciliatory gesture. "How well I know. But your services are the best, first class."

Pluchenko nodded, turning to Rashid. "You tell Kamal that I can guarantee him at least one submarine voyage. It will cost him twenty million dollars, deposited in advance to my Swiss account. Any additional excursions will be an additional ten million, also in advance."

"We have a deal," Rashid said.

Pluchenko filled a tall glass with vodka and raised it to Rashid's tea-cup.

Reza Deghani narrowed his eyes at his two associates.

Several couples danced close to where the trio sat, and one of them brushed against the back of Pluchenko's seat. The soft music, a tango, brought a smile to Pluchenko's lips and he turned to watch the young couples.

When the dance was over, Pluchenko rose and shook Rashid's hand. "I'll leave the negotiations on the chemicals to Reza. But send my regards to Kamal. Tell him the submarine will be ready soon."

He turned to Deghani and they embraced. Deghani planted a kiss on each of Pluchenko's cheeks. Then the Russian made his way across the dance floor, where couples had begun to waltz.

Reza Deghani watched him go then returned his attention to Rashid. "I am sorry you are not interested in my deal with your lady friend. It requires me to negotiate for chemicals with others and perhaps convince our friend Pluchenko to offer the submarine to another client."

"What other client?"

"Iran. They have a use for it too. It delivers an unbelievably massive nuclear punch, you know. And, unfortunately, there is only one at the moment. The other kilo class submarines are either under repair or in mothballs for lack of funds to refurbish them. I guarantee that Iran is prepared to offer the Russians a larger sum for it."

"You are crazy, Reza, but not stupid. I tell you what. I have a better deal than your countrymen."

"Tell me."

"The one I'm offering will allow you to live and to do it with all limbs intact."

"I see."

"Here's what I have in mind."

# CHAPTER 14

Linda stood at the window, open to the hot desert wind. Mustafa, the hotel clerk and an assistant had taken over her room, supposedly to fix her toilet.

Finally, she climbed out onto the fire escape and into Roger's window adjacent to her room. It was early and he was still asleep, despite the hot wind blowing through his fourth floor hotel suite identical to hers. At least, that's what the hotel clerk downstairs had called them when they checked in. Suites. What a joke, Linda thought as she watched Roger peacefully sprawled on the narrow bed, oblivious to her or the heat.

The hotel clerk had promised queen-size replacements, but never came through with them, despite Roger's warning that the hotel manager would be informed.

"He probably is the hotel manager," Linda had told him.

The cry of a muezzin began the morning call to prayer from a mosque nearby. Linda looked out the window at the tall minaret rising above the mosque's roof, to where the muezzin stood calling the faithful. Then another one joined the first, then another, until Linda could hear hundreds, perhaps a thousand of muezzin voices, screaming together in concert.

Then in the manner it had begun, one voice fell away, then another, until only one muezzin's voice hung in the air from the direction of the Nile. Then like the rest of the muezzin calls, it too ended. Then silence.

Despite all this, Roger slept, and now lay on his side. Linda could see his handsome face against the pillow.

She turned back to the window, looking west toward the desert. Its smell and others—rotting garbage, dust, donkey dung, burning wood, and the exhaust fumes from thousands of cars and trucks—were carried in with the heat and wind.

Both their air conditioners were broken, despite the clerk's other promise that they would be fixed soon. Linda guessed that they had never worked, at least not for years. "Inshalla," he had said. She closed the shutters and the room became somewhat cooler with the wind blocked.

She tiptoed back toward the bed and watched Roger turn to his former position on the pillow. She yanked the pillow out from under him.

"You're up already?" Roger said, sitting up suddenly.

"You must have been tired. You slept right through all that bedlam outside."

He looked at his watch, and shook his head. "What the hell are you doing in my room? Not that I mind," he said flirtatiously.

"They're fixing my toilet."

A loud knock on the door interrupted her. Roger shouted, "Who is it?"

"It's Mustafa, the hotel clerk. Ya-Saidi. I come to fix your toilet."

Both Linda and Roger burst out laughing. "All right, Mustafa. You come back in half an hour."

"Sure, Ya-Saidi," Mustafa said.

"I'll shower and we'll go find some breakfast," Roger said to Linda. "Unless you have something else in mind."

"Nope, breakfast sounds good. I'm going back to my room to wait." Linda went to the window, opened the shutters, and started through.

"Do you always go in and out through windows?"

"I didn't have your key," she said and disappeared.

# CHAPTER 15

The road from El Giza and the pyramids took them through Helwan toward the desert and to the paratroop base at Bir Gindali.

Roger drove the rental car, a Renault, on the narrow desert road in silence, marveling at the vast spread of sand dunes stretching toward the mountains. Few vehicles traveled the road this late afternoon; and Roger knew they would have to travel in darkness to get back to Cairo that night, but he had to take the chance.

Linda sat in the passenger seat, looking at the changing scenery. Two buzzards circled a corpse in the sand, perhaps a dead hyena.

"So, what's the deal between Leah and Mark?" Roger asked.

"The deal?"

"You know what I mean, are they an *Item*?"

Linda laughed. "Your advanced age is showing."

"What! That's not the way to put it?"

"Not these days."

"How's this: Is Mark jumping her bones?"

Now Linda really laughed. "Oh my, god, you're funny."

"Well, how the hell would you say it, Ms. Cool?"

"I wouldn't ask. It's none of our business."

"Oh, but you can be so irritating."

"I say she's in love with Ben."

"That Israeli Alpha commando?"

"That's the one."

"So, what's wrong with Mark?"

"Boring, maybe."

"Oh, so you women like us action guys."

"Some do."

"And you?"

"I go for the professors."

"What did I just say, you're just plain irritating."

She grinned. "So, do you think Al-Sharif will be there?"

He squinted, shielding his eyes from the strong sun, just past high noon, arching toward the Mediterranean. "It's a long shot, but what the hell. So far, he's stayed one jump ahead of us. I just hope we'll be able to get into the paratroop base."

The long drive in the desert heat had parched Linda's lips. She yearned for the comfort of the hotel room, which now seemed like heaven. They passed a sign pointing to a dirt road. Ahead, the paratroop base appeared to rise out of the shimmering desert floor like a mirage. When they reached the gate, a husky paratrooper raised his hand, signaling them to stop.

"What is your business here?" the sentry inquired in fairly good English.

"We were invited by your commander to attend the paratroopers' reunion," Roger said with a straight face.

Linda squirmed.

"Can I see your papers?" the sentry asked.

Roger handed him his passport and a special permit he'd received from the embassy for this very purpose. After a lengthy examination, the sentry handed the papers back. "You are fortunate," he said, looking at Linda with curiosity. "The ceremonies have just ended, but the main show is going to begin shortly. A paratroop drop of over five hundred commandos."

"That's impressive," Roger said, looking toward the interior of the base where a crowd had gathered in the distance.

"You can go in," the sentry said, smiling at Linda. Roger noticed the AK-47 in his large hands. He lifted the gate pole and Roger waved and drove through. They parked the vehicle in a designated area and walked toward the gathering.

They seemed to be the only foreigners there. Both civilians and enlisted men stood around talking in rapid Arabic, sometimes hugging each other like long lost brethren. Roger scanned the crowd, but there was no sign of Rashid Al-Sharif. He had either been here earlier or they had simply been given incorrect information.

Roger nodded to Linda in frustration. They circled among the guests, tasting the food and drink, mingling with the men and the few women who eyed them with suspicion.

"Do you know Rashid Al-Sharif?" Roger asked a man who introduced himself as Muhammad Al-Zeitun.

"Yes, of course," Al-Zeitun said smiling at Linda. She felt him devouring her with his black shining eyes.

"Have you seen him here today?"

"Yes." He was here a few hours ago during the ceremonies. But he had a flight to catch."

"So, you spoke to him?"

"Yes, I did. He is an old acquaintance. We served together in the paratroopers before he went to America."

Roger nodded, looking at Linda. "Well, I guess we can leave," he said to her.

"What about the show, the paratroop drop? Aren't you staying?" Al-Zeitun asked.

"I am sorry," Roger answered, "we must return to Cairo tonight."

"You are from the American Embassy." It was not a question.

"No. Actually, we were hoping to see Rashid. He is an old acquaintance of mine also. They told me at the embassy that I might find him here. Have you known him long?"

Al-Zeitun smiled, nodding. "Yes. You know, he rose in rank to a major."

"Is Rashid's former commanding officer still at this base?" Roger asked.

"He's retired," Al-Zeitun answered, "but he is here today."

"Would you point him out to me?"

"It would be my pleasure, in fact, let me introduce you to him."

They walked toward a group of men, some in civilian clothes, but most wearing uniforms. Roger noticed a few high-ranking officers among them. Al-Zeitun went over to a husky gray-haired man of medium height and spoke to him in rapid Arabic. Then he turned to Roger. "I would like you to meet our commander, General Ali Fahmi."

The retired general shook Roger's hand warmly.

"My assistant, Linda Ashcroft," Roger said and the general shook her hand next.

"It's a pleasure meeting you, General," Roger said. "I have heard a lot about you as commander of this elite unit."

"Have you now?" General Fahmi seemed surprised. He spoke in a perfect, clipped British accent.

"I have my sources," Roger said, smiling.

"Can I be of any help to you?"

"I was hoping to see Rashid Al-Sharif, but I understand that he already left," Roger said, frustration in his voice.

"So, you know him?" the general asked.

"Yes. May I have a word with you in private, General?"

Fahmi looked at Roger with curiosity. "Yes, of course. Why don't we walk," he said, pointing toward the neat rows of army tents almost touching the desert sand.

Roger whispered to Linda and she nodded. "Would you mind showing Ms. Ashcroft around?" he asked Al-Zeitun. The man's face lit up and he led Linda off across the grounds to find a good spot to view the paratroopers who would soon fill the sky.

"So, what's on your mind?" General Fahmi asked.

"May I speak frankly, General?"

"Of course."

"It's about Rashid Al-Sharif. How well do you know him?"

The question caught Fahmi by surprise. "Are you asking me whether I knew him while he served under my command?"

"Yes, and whether you know of his activities these days."

"I see," Fahmi said. He hesitated. "I can tell you that he was an outstanding paratrooper. I even recommended him for additional training at Fort Bragg in the States. When he returned, we used him to recruit informants for intelligence purposes. Later, of course, he approached the CIA and even worked for them."

Roger recalled that all this was documented in Rashid's thick file. "So, you are not aware of his activities at this time?"

"Well," the general told him, "we hear rumors. But of course, I treat them as such. I did ask Rashid today about some of them, but he only shrugged and flashed that disarming smile of his. I hear the rascal is very good with the ladies."

"Yes, I suppose he is. Obviously, I was hoping to see him while I was in the area. Too bad it didn't work out."

"Yes," Fahmi said, "he had to catch a flight to Europe."

"Did he say where?"

"Evidently, he had several stops to make, one of them is London. Can I help you in any other way?"

"Yes, in fact," Roger said, handing him a card. "My private phone number is on the card. You can reach me any time, day or night. I'd appreciate any further information you might learn about Rashid."

The general nodded and offered his hand. "When you get back to the States, please give my regards to John Devine, will you?"

"You know John Devine?"

General Fahmi smiled. "Shall I say we are old acquaintances? I met John when he was serving in the Sinai Desert with the first units that arrived after the peace treaty with Israel."

"You should have mentioned that when we first met," Roger joked.

"You didn't ask," Fahmi answered with a broad grin.

# CHAPTER 16

The first missile hit the side of the mountain, exploding with a thunderous force. It threw the occupants of the cave toward its craggy walls, injuring most of them. The rest lay on the cave floor, dead or dying.

Other caves had been hit too. The only structures outside, a long wooden table and the shed above it, were burning in the inferno that followed.

Miles away, Kamal was startled from his prayers when suddenly the far mountains lit up, followed by loud explosions that echoed through the ravines and canyons.

Immediately, his cellular phone rang and he took it out of the pocket of his robe. "Yes?" he said, tersely.

"Ya Rais, we are under attack. It is terrible here. Many are dead. More are injured. It must be the Americans. They've found our base."

"Calm down, do you hear me, Shafiq? This is the price we must pay for our work. Let the Americans come. We will show them again and again what we can do. You go and help your people, and Allah be with you."

The line went dead and Kamal cursed under his breath. He would be on the run again, atop a camel in a caravan heading eastward, away from his base.

Those who survived would follow him. The struggle would continue. Should he risk calling Rashid, or should he e-mail him when he got the chance?

It was imperative that Rashid complete his assignment, Kamal reminded himself. In fact, he would put him in charge of the entire operation, for he was the most suitable man and spoke fluent English.

———

Hours later, the movements of his camel lulled Kamal into a restless sleep and his mind wandered. He envisioned his dead father calling his name. But only the memory of him was left, a memory of weakness, and a legacy of empty platitudes.

His father had been a generous, spiritual man, indeed, albeit misguided. He did not share his son's vision of a world governed by Muslim rule. "Not if it means violence, bloodshed, and loss of freedom for others," he once told Kamal during a bitter argument.

The harsh sound of heavy explosions jolted him. He saw the bright orange glow again and cursed, then shouted to the caravan leader to move ahead toward the new hiding place. He pulled his cellular out of his black robe and punched a button.

"Aywah," a voice said.

"Is everything ready?"

"Yes, Ya Rais. We are ready. We have everything and only await transportation."

His call had surprised Rashid. He heard it in his voice. "So, we're on target?" Kamal asked.

"Yes, prepared for delivery."

"I will wire payment directly, as discussed," Kamal promised him.

"I trust you, Ya Rais. Thank you." Rashid's voice faded, as a third explosion echoed in the far mountains, sending another cloud of fire across the dark mountains.

When Kamal spoke again the line was dead. He shouted at the

caravan leader: "Back to the base!" They would help the people there, if any had survived the bombardment.

The caravan leader nodded in the dark and turned his camel around. The rest of the caravan did the same.

In the hypnotizing shadows of the night, his mind wandered. In his mind's eye, a woman caressed his face. He sighed. Kamal missed the softness of his mistress, but she was far away from this desolated wind-swept plateau. Another flash of orange illuminated the far mountains beneath the pale moon. An explosion followed and he cursed again.

# CHAPTER 17

Heavy sheets of rain pelted the windshield obscuring visibility on the wet road ahead. They were on the Autostrada and Ben could see an occasional red tail light shine through the heavy downpour. He and Uri, who was driving, had left Bologna before dawn. Though they had craved an extra hour of sleep, they couldn't afford the time.

"I hope Leah will be there," Ben said as he watched the brake lights of a fast-moving Mercedes disappear again. He had hardly seen Leah since she'd teamed with Mark Lindsey, her former biology professor at Harvard. They had been doing research together on the immediate-and long term-effects of anthrax. They were working on an antidote, an agent to rival the one being developed by the British company, A. G. Hitchcock, Ltd.

"She promised," Uri said.

"When did you talk to her?"

"Day before yesterday."

Ben concentrated on the treacherous road as though he were driving. They were fast approaching the outskirts of Milan, on their way to the Bergamo Airport. "Did she say anything about the research?"

"Only that they've been hard at it."

"When is the flight to Israel due to leave Bergamo?"

"We will have two hours to spare," Uri said, looking at his watch.

"Good, then we don't have to speed so." Uri's driving was making him tense.

"And have someone run over us?" Uri answered, making it clear that he did not appreciate the advice.

Uri did slow down finally, though the only indication of it was that other cars now passed them on the right. Then, after several encounters with impatient drivers who honked or flashed headlights they could barely see in the downpour, Uri abandoned the fast lane. Despite that, he maintained a ninety-five-mile-an-hour pace on the slick, dangerous road.

"I spoke to Aaron Golan last night," Ben said, interrupting his own paranoia about the drive.

"How's he doing?"

"His usual self. As busy as Leah."

"Yeah, hard workers those Golans."

Suddenly the rain stopped. The outskirts of Milan came into view at the end of a long curve, and they could see the large road signs and their arrows pointing to Bergamo and Venezzia. "We're on the final leg," Uri said.

Yes, thank god. Ben would be more than relieved to leave behind the Autostrada and the breakneck speeds of those who drove it.

Leah was waiting for them at the airport lounge when they arrived. Ben hugged her to him and felt her body tense for a moment. He let go of his hold and kissed her gently on the forehead. He had not meant to push himself on her this way and he regretted doing so.

"You look wonderful," he told her, and she did. "It's been a while."

"Yes," she said, smiling at him.

"How was your flight?"

"Uneventful. I flew non-stop to Milan. Thanks for your help, Ben. It's nice to fly first class."

"You can thank Uri here. He's in charge of transportation in our department."

Leah looked at Ben, noticing his bulging arms. "You've been doing some weight lifting."

"Not lately. Unfortunately, in this line of work, one must be thankful for even the smallest opportunity to work out in a decent gym."

They headed in the direction of the airport lobby, where a large group of Italian nuns going to the holy land waited for the same El-Al flight they would be on.

"I think we have over an hour before we board," Ben said. "Why don't we get some coffee?"

"A good idea," Uri said. "I'm famished."

Ben eyed him. "You just had a sandwich when we stopped for gas."

"Two hours ago," Uri exclaimed.

Ben smiled at him and winked at Leah. "Uri is a growing boy."

Leah put her arm around Uri. She had known him since they were young students at the regional high school in upper Galilee. "Uri has always been hungry," she said, and kissed his cheek.

When they reached the airport cafeteria, Ben noticed that it was almost empty. Two priests were sitting at a corner table having coffee and an Italian air stewardess sat near them with a croissant.

They took a table at the far corner and ordered coffee, sandwiches and chips. After the waiter left, Ben turned to Leah. "Your father can hardly wait to see you and, of course, hear about your research."

"Good, we have a few developments that might please him."

"Tell us," Ben said.

"Well, you know, we've been trying to find an antidote for the anthrax bacteria. But I'm sure you two know more about anthrax than I do."

She looked directly at Ben, almost flirtatiously, he thought. "Not me. I know more about who has it than about the stuff itself."

"Well, it's sometimes called the poor man's atomic bomb. A silent killer, extremely lethal."

"So that's why it's used for germ warfare?" Uri asked.

"There are several reasons. Its spores can be produced in large quantities and stored for decades with just a basic knowledge of biology, using relatively unsophisticated equipment. And the spores are easily spread by projectiles and sprayers."

"You mean it can be fired from missiles or sprayed from aircraft?" Ben asked.

"Yes," Leah said. "Even from hand-held aerosols. And just five pounds of it can wipe out half the population of Washington, DC, for example. There is no cloud or color to it. No smell, taste, boom or bang—and no effective treatment for unvaccinated victims."

"What about antibiotics?" Uri asked.

"They'll suppress infection if administered before symptoms occur, usually within the first 24 to 48 hours. But there's only a one-percent chance of survival without them."

"How come the spores last so long? Don't bacteria die easily?" Ben asked.

"This one has an extremely tough protective coat. Yet it only takes one to six days to incubate."

"So, if you inhale it, you're dead," Uri said.

"Highly likely, because the spores migrate to the lymph nodes, change to bacteria, multiply, and produce toxins that destroy the structure of the middle chest."

"So, what's the answer, gas masks?" he asked.

"Actually, you can be infected by ingesting contaminated meat or by contact with diseased animals or animal products. But the inhalation of spores is by far the most-deadly. Death can occur within 24 to 36 hours."

"Quite an horror," Uri said.

"Yes," Ben agreed. "And to think that at least ten countries are developing it for warfare, among them, the Iranians."

"We're getting close to an antidote," Leah said quietly. "I believe a breakthrough is imminent."

Ben just stared at her. She was so impressive. How could he ever compete with that brilliant man heading this important project?

"So, you're working with that scientist?" Uri asked.

"Yes, Mark Lindsey, my former professor at Harvard. He's quite an expert on the subject."

Ben frowned. Obviously, he didn't have a chance.

Just then they heard the airport intercom announcing the boarding of El-Al Flight 03 to Tel-Aviv.

"By the way. What were you two doing in Bologna?" she asked.

"Company business," Ben said, looking at Uri. Of course, he could not tell Leah that they were on the trail of an international terrorist named Aldo Gardini, who had once attended the university there.

In Tel Aviv that night, he and Leah went alone to dinner. Afterwards they walked leisurely back to their hotel along a street of sidewalk cafes. Unexpectedly, she took his arm. He smiled down at her. "I've missed you."

"That goes for me too," she said shyly.

"That surprises me."

"Why?"

"I thought you were in love with Mark Lindsey."

"Maybe that's just a passing thing. You know, that old student-gets-crush-on-professor syndrome."

They were near the hotel now and they stood at a window display of roses at a florist shop to its right. "I hope that's what it is . . . or was."

She blushed.

He didn't know what to say. "When you're sure it's over with him, will you let me know?"

"Yes," she said.

He kissed her. Just the smell of her was overwhelming. Leah Golan, the woman he had loved for years.

# CHAPTER 18

The victory march of Guiseppi Verde's Aida thundered toward its climax, punctuated by the deep voice of Ramfis, the Egyptian High Priest, and the dance before the Goddess Isis.

Ben smiled at Leah next to him, her face aglow as she watched the unfolding story of Aida's love for Radames. It had truly been a marvelous evening, he thought.

Their dinner prior to the opera had been superb, and Leah kept talking about the future, one that apparently included him, from what she said. She mentioned that she would like to show him the 9/11 Site in New York and the remarkable clean-up and memorial plans. She said that in the morning she'd like to drive to an area outside the city so he could meet her elderly aunt. She told him he would love a certain painting she'd bought in Rome, and so on. All of it had been music to his ears and he'd barely eaten.

The voice of Radames, the Egyptian warrior cut through his thoughts as the famous opera tenor, Placido Domingo, portraying Radames, sang his song of victory over Aida's father, defeated King of Ethiopia.

Ben looked at Leah and smiled. His love and affection for her grew stronger all the time. Just thinking about it sent a chill through him. He guessed it was this incredible possibility of happiness with Leah that made him suddenly afraid of disaster intervening. Though it was inconceivable to him that some hostile regime might attempt to attack or blackmail his country with instruments of mass death, evidence to the contrary was everywhere.

Leah touched his hand, drawing him back to the opera. The Egyptian High Priest was warning the King of Egypt not to release the Ethiopian prisoners of war. Ben began to relax again and put his mind on the unfolding story of Aida. He took Leah's hand and held it. She squeezed back gently. Then he felt the cell phone in his jacket pocket vibrate.

Ben leaned over to Leah and whispered where to meet him at the next intermission. He got up and excused himself as he squeezed by the other opera patrons in the row. Once in the lobby, he told the usher he would return shortly and hurried outside. He punched the cell phone talk button.

"Yes?" he said.

"It's Aaron Golan."

Ben shot a worried look behind him, to make sure that no one was following him. Golan's voice thundered in his ear. "Sorry to bother you at the opera. But are you two all right?"

"Yes, why?"

"I don't know. I just had this crazy urge to call."

"Do you want me to have Leah call you during intermission?"

"No, no, I think I'm just turning into an old . . ." General Golan's voice faded.

"Aaron, I'm losing you. Are you still there?"

Leah's father's voice came back suddenly. "You be careful, and give my love to Leah. Keep her out of harm's way."

"I promise you. She's in safe hands."

"I know. I trust you implicitly."

Ben heard a click and he folded the cellular and tucked it into his jacket pocket. He lifted his jacket collar against a cold wind blowing from the direction of the sea and walked briskly back toward the opera house to Leah and his favorite opera. Still her father's concern was disturbing. Was there something he hadn't wanted to tell them? Ben knew things were coming to a head. The CIA had already mounted a world-wide search for Rashid Al-Sharif and Ibn-Sultan, similar to the one launched for Bin-Laden. He knew American bombers were flying over Afghanistan again, in search of their headquarters.

When he entered the lobby, crowds began to stream out into the vestibule for intermission and he saw Leah coming towards him. She took his hand and pulled him aside.

She looked him square in the eyes. "You asked me the other day if I had gotten over Mark Lindsey and I told you I would let you know when I was sure."

"I remember."

"I am absolutely certain," she said and kissed his cheek. That was the last thing he remembered before the blood curdling explosion and wall of fire—those words—ones he had so longed to hear, and the touch of her lips on his cheek.

His next memory was her father at his bedside. "I am so sorry, Ben," Aaron Golan said, tears running down his cheeks.

"Leah?"

Her father looked away. "I know how much you loved her."

# CHAPTER 19

Linda and Roger took a train into London from the airport, still on Rashid Al-Sharif's trail. Linda was only too happy to see a cold fog roll in from the sea in a dense blanket over the city. Roger left her at the hotel on his way to the embassy. She showered and ordered some tea, wishing for a really good cup of coffee. She sat on the bed with her laptop and went through their e-mail. Al-Sharif had disappeared but Reza Deghani had been seen at a cafe popular with Mid-Easterners in London. Her guess was that he was contacting someone from A. C. Hitchcock right here in the city.

After she had answered her mail, downloaded some maps, and finished some research, she turned on the news. She listened attentively to one segment, a discussion of a possible peace treaty between the Israelis and Palestinians, perhaps possible now that new leadership had taken over both nations' political machines. It looked as unlikely as ever, according to one member of the House of Commons speaking before the news cameras.

There was a knock on the door. "Who is it?" she called.

"It's me, ready to take you to dinner."

She opened the door. "Hey," she said. "So early?"

"We'll do a few errands on the way."

She laughed. They were always doing a few errands on the way and as often as not, ended up not getting any dinner. She grabbed a coat, knowing how chilly an evening in fog could get.

On the way out, she stopped to buy a newspaper in the hotel lobby. When they got into the cab, she scanned the headlines. She pointed to an article. "I heard this on the news earlier. The whole thing's ironic," she said.

"What's is?"

"The Holly Land. The seat of a major religion continually fought over by two other major religions, and none of them looking very impressive. The Islamic extremists are terrorists, killing women and children. The Holy Roman Church and its affiliates are still trying to recover from the scandal of hiding its own sins against children. It's enough to make you wonder about the institution of religion. I imagine the great souls who inspired these sects are crying somewhere over the great spiritual divide to see how their followers have misinterpreted their messages, in order to serve political corruption and monetary greed."

Roger laughed. "Spiritual divide. Huh? Is that sort of like the continental divide?"

"Sort of," she said, smacking him with her newspaper.

"You are an interesting woman, Linda."

"Yes, now if I could just find an interesting guy."

"Hey, no fly fishing for you! Ignoring the possibilities, before you like you do."

"Possibilities, hah! I don't want to hear any more about your damn fly-fishing. You are so full of bologna."

"You'll see."

Linda laughed and went back to her newspaper.

When they got back to the hotel, they made plans to leave early the next morning to check out a few places where Victor Shalyapin had last been seen. Roger left her at her door and Linda undressed and got ready for bed. She'd just come out of the bathroom when she heard a knock on the door. "Who is it?" she asked.

"It's me."

She put on her robe and opened the door, already feeling that something was wrong. Roger's face told her she was right. "May I come, for a minute?"

She closed the door behind him. "What's wrong?"

"It's Leah."

"Oh, my God," she cried, holding her hand to her mouth.

She sat down on the bed and he sat beside her. He took her hand. "She was killed at the opera tonight by a suicide bomber. She was with Ben Shamir and he was taken to the hospital......"

"Oh, please Roger. Tell me that's not true. Tell me that Leah is OK."

He set quietly, holding her hand."

"I can't stand this," Linda sobbed. "The craziness never ends."

"I know."

Linda couldn't hold back her tears and Roger held her. "She was the best person I've ever known. She was . . ." Linda couldn't finish and Roger wiped her tears with his hand. Finally, without letting go of her, he lay back with her against the pillows and she cried herself to sleep in his arms.

The next morning, Linda's head was on his chest. They were still on top of the covers, Linda in her robe and Roger in the clothes he had worn to dinner.

"Are you okay?" he asked her.

"No," she said, "I have a terrible headache." She got up and went into the bathroom and he heard the shower.

"I'll be back," Roger hollered through the bathroom door before leaving. He went up a floor to his own room to shower, then down to the restaurant off the lobby. Linda's devastation over Leah had touched him. All of a sudden, she was so vulnerable, so fragile, and his heart went out to her.

He ordered breakfast for two and returned to her room with a tray of coffee, fruit, toast and eggs. Once she let him in, he put the tray on the table and put his arms around her.

"Thank you," she said. He realized she was touched by his concern for her, and that it was making her cry again. He kissed her gently and she responded. Suddenly he knew he didn't want to spend his life without her and that keeping her safe and happy seemed like the most important thing he had ever wanted to do, and the most meaningful.

# CHAPTER 20

A light breeze moved the dusty curtains, as the tide rose along the shoreline of Sidon. The strong smell of salt air wafted into the room where Kamal Ibn-Sultan lay on the bed. He inhaled deeply of the delicious scent that he had always loved.

Next to him, Lila stirred. Her dark thick hair spread on the pillow was in contrast to her white naked body beside him.

He looked at her firm breasts, resting against his side, and he smiled. Lila was a good lover and the only woman he really cared for. His infrequent visits to this seaport town only heightened the desire he had for her.

He took a Turkish cigarette out of the pack on the night table and lit it. Lila stirred again, turned on her back and opened one eye. She smiled.

He patted her head then sank his fingers into her dark, lush hair. He caressed her breasts and squeezed her nipples lightly. She moved and wrapped her legs around him.

They listened to the cries of the seagulls outside, their fierce competition for the few dead fish on the empty quay intensifying.

Kamal pulled her beneath him and, when she opened her legs, mounted her. She cried out to him and his strokes inside her heightened. After they'd climaxed, Kamal fell exhausted beside her still quivering body. He lay in blissful silence, listening to the sound of the breaking waves outside.

The cellular phone on the table rang and Kamal reached across the bed for it. He was expecting Rashid's call.

"Ya Rais," Rashid's voice came on the line. "Is this a good time?"

Kamal could hear the noise of moving vehicles in the background. "Yes, go ahead." Lila stirred and he got out of bed and stood naked at the window, watching waves furiously attacking the jetty.

"We have the blueprint."

"Good, your contractor found an architect?" Kamal said, watching gulls diving into the sea for fish.

"Yes, in England."

"Very well, friend," Kamal said as he turned to look at Lila going toward the bathroom, her straight lush figure and tight buttocks moving away from him. "And how about delivery of the building materials?"

"Everything is arranged. I'm going to Zurich, day after tomorrow to make sure that qualified laborers will be on site as scheduled."

"Did you arrange for funding?" Kamal inquired.

"Yes. I'll make the down payment in Bellagio."

"Good, you are an excellent foreman and will receive a handsome paycheck this quarter."

"Thank you, Ya Rais."

Rashid's voice faded, but then, came back, stronger. "One more thing. There's this man again. Our competitor. He has been trailing me for quite some time now. My sources in Egypt inform me that he was looking for me there only an hour after I left."

"What were you doing in Egypt?"

"I stopped on my way to Europe."

"A foolish move."

"It was just a nostalgic visit."

"A visit that could have disrupted our plans and endangered your project."

"But nothing happened. Allah protects."

"Yes," Kamal said, his voice calmer, "but I know that man. I have some of my people in the States checking him out. A dangerous man, they are telling me."

"I will be careful."

"Yes, be sure that you are, and after you have finished with the business at hand, meet me in Lebanon in the Bekaa Valley at the usual place, yes?"

"Yes, surely."

Kamal hung up and folded the cellular phone. He turned his gaze from the window to Lila now wearing a long white robe, open down the front. He could see her breasts sway under the thin cloth. He felt excited again and went toward her.

# CHAPTER 21

"As you know, the town of Al-Hirmil is sitting astride the Bekaa Valley, almost at the tip of it," said General Golan, pointing to a spot on the map pinned to the wall behind his desk. He turned slowly to Ben, standing beside him. "What do you think? Does my plan make sense so far?"

"It all depends," he said to the retired general, on loan from the Defense Ministry as an advisor to the Mossad's special Alpha Team, which Ben headed. Golan looked at him with sad, puzzled eyes.

"On what?"

"It might not be easy to get my men in and out of the Bekaa Valley. The place is swarming with Syrian troops, Hezbollah terrorists, PLO renegades and other riffraff, not to mention the Syrian and Lebanese drug lords who actually control the valley."

"But my plan is a good one. You have to admit that," the General insisted.

Ben looked at the map. The Bekaa Valley was nestled between tall mountains with the Litani River running its entire length between them. On one such mission to Al-Hirmil, many years ago it seemed now, his team had brought a terrorist leader back with them. It had been a daring commando raid, Ben remembered, for the leader was part of a group that had moved a nuclear-tipped missile into the town of Jericho in order to blow the fragile peace treaty that his country had signed with the Palestinians.

"So, what do you think, Ben? I need your opinion. I promised the Americans an answer by tonight."

"Feasible, but perilous," Ben said at last, "like our last visit to Al-Hirmil. You surely remember it, don't you Aaron?"

"I do," Golan said.

"This will be every bit as difficult," Ben added, suddenly thinking of Leah. She'd been on his mind those nights even way back then. By the way Golan was looking at him, Ben knew the older man was thinking of her too. For the moment Ben couldn't look at him and returned his gaze to the map.

The emotions and the memories were unbearable.

"There is another problem though," Ben said, regaining his composure. "We will have to ferry our commandos to the top of the Jebel Lubnan mountain range where it slopes toward Al-Hirmil."

"It resembles the plan we used in the past," Golan reminded him.

"Yes, but that time we did not have to rendezvous with an American team," Ben said quietly. "It complicates things."

"It's a matter of coordination. The Americans will fly their commando team by helicopter from a carrier off the Lebanese coast. They can meet our team on top of the mountain plateau, yes?" Golan asked.

Ben thought it over. "Your plan is workable, Aaron. You can tell the Americans we will be ready for them. But I would like to meet their team commander."

"I can arrange that," Golan assured him. "We can deliver you to their carrier."

Ben nodded. "What do you hear from the Americans?"

Golan smiled dryly. "I spoke to an old acquaintance in Washington yesterday who says Rashid Al-Sharif was spotted in Egypt, talking to some of the outlawed Islamic fundamentalists involved in the assassination of Answar Sadat."

Ben shot a curious look at him. "Didn't one of our men spot Al-Sharif in Zurich getting on a train?"

"Yes, but someone in a van picked him up at the station in Como and by the time our man there found a cab, there was no trace of him."

"A real fuck-up," Ben said quietly, looking at Aaron.

"Yes," Aaron agreed, "but the Americans picked up his trail again in Bellagio where he met with Gregory Pluchenko. My source says something is in the works."

"Any information about Ibn-Sultan?"

"We have reliable information that he will meet Al-Sharif at a villa belonging to a local Hezbollah leader in Al-Hirmil."

"So that's why you need the Alpha Team. You have something more in mind."

Golan smiled as he studied the map. Then he began detailing the rest of his plan.

# CHAPTER 22

The men crawled down toward the valley on this chilly, damp night, through mist and patches of heavy fog. In the west, clouds drifted across a sliver of moon.

Ben clutched the Heckler & Koch MP5 to his chest and raised one hand. The commando behind him caught the sign and signaled to the men behind him to halt.

Above the ridge, they saw the silhouettes of men in a military maneuver, walking just above them. It seemed to Ben that it had to be a Syrian army unit, perhaps returning from a night patrol in the Bekaa Valley below.

The column of soldiers suddenly stopped. Ben heard the sound of liquid against the rocks, as some of the Syrians urinated, barely twenty feet away from him.

He raised his hand again, this time lifting his weapon and crossing it with his other hand, and the man behind him understood and signaled the commandos behind him to hold their fire until the very last moment.

Moments later, one of the patrol soldiers began telling his companions a joke and the men burst into a roar of laughter. Ben joined them silently. He understood their language and appreciated their humor. Even here, in the rugged mountains overlooking the Bekaa

Valley, the world didn't stop. The Syrians were enjoying their comrade's story about the former president of the United States and a cigar.

Ben thought of the beleaguered ex-president and his resiliency, and smiled in the darkness.

After the laughter died down, a harsh voice, probably their commanding officer's, reminded the Syrians not to break the silence again, though the juicy details of the joke had made him laugh too.

The soldiers marched on, leaving Ben and his team of commandos, a curious mix. Three-fourths were from the Mossad Alpha Team and the rest from the US Special Delta Force, brought in by helicopter from an American aircraft carrier off the coast of Cyprus.

Ben rose and the lead scout took the point again and the rest of the commandos followed in his footsteps. He looked at his watch and lifted its protective plastic cover. The phosphorus hands showed that they had already marched non-stop for almost four hours since the helicopter landing.

Eric LaGrange, the Delta Force commander was a seasoned battle-scarred veteran, presently marching with his troops parallel to Ben's force of elite commandos. Ben knew that the caves overlooking the approaches to Al-Hirmil were an hour away. He had been here before, and although the moon was hidden beyond the drifting clouds, he remembered the rugged mountainous terrain. He caught up to the lead scout and whispered, "Avi, we must hurry, it's almost dawn."

Avi nodded and began to move faster. The commandos increased their pace too, careful to avoid the large dark boulders scattered in their path. They didn't dare let a weapon strike the boulders and send up the unmistakable ring of metal on granite through the vast mountain passes.

In the pre-dawn light, the town of Al-Hirmil and its spread of stone houses could be seen reaching into the foothills of the mountains that dwarfed it. Pink sheets suddenly appeared from the east and the dark mountains, outlined against the dark sky, slowly lightened. The fog still drifted inside the canyons and crevices leading toward Al-Hirmil.

A rooster cried and its voice carried through the crisp mountain air as the last of the commandos found shelter inside the large cave overlooking the valley. Two sentries stood guard outside, hiding behind a large boulder, their camouflaged battle dress blending with the rugged terrain, as they shielded their eyes from the rising sun.

Ben held his flashlight over the map spread across the cave floor. He pointed out a spot on it for Eric LaGrange. "This is where the villa is located. We'll rest here today and take turns guarding the cave. We'll leave four men on watch and rotate them every two hours. Then at midnight, we'll move out."

Eric nodded. "A good plan."

"The Bekaa Valley is a dangerous place," Ben added. "I was here once on another mission. We were lucky than, I hope we're lucky now."

"What happened?" Eric asked, and the commandos gathered around.

"Some renegade PLO group moved nuclear-tipped missiles into Jericho and we were here to capture one of their leaders. We came in the same way as last night."

"I remember that crisis," Eric said. "We were on full alert." He smiled at Ben. "Then PLO renegades blocked the Lincoln Tunnel in Manhattan during a Friday evening rush hour."

"Yes, that was after we blew up their missile launcher at Jericho. It was all a part of the same scheme. We were lucky. It could have ended in tragedy."

Eric nodded, as the men around them came closer, huddling together in the chilly cave.

"So, here's how we're going to do it," Ben said, pointing at the map. "Eric, your commandos will be our blocking force. We will approach the villa from the north. This route is almost impassable, according to the map. There is a steep canyon almost all the way to the villa. It's covered with thick growth, mostly pine, and will provide good protection from probing eyes."

Ben paused, looking at each of the warriors around him. "Your commandos will approach from the west. This is where their reinforcements will arrive once they hear any shooting. So, let's do our utmost to take our targets out without noise. Don't forget that the place is crawling with Syrian troops as well as terrorists, Hezbollah, PLO renegade groups, and God knows what else." He paused to look over at Eric.

"So, you guys be careful. This is the real thing. According to our source, both Kamal Ibn-Sultan and Rashid Al-Sharif are holed up in the villa. You might call it a conference of devils."

The men smiled. They liked Ben, his straight talk and dry humor. He was a real leader, and the American team respected his knowledge and experience.

They carried RPG launchers, H&K MP5's, and plenty of ammunition in their backpacks, as well as hand grenades and other equipment. Each wore a stubby commando knife. They were the best that the U.S. and the Israeli army had to offer, all veterans of combat.

Eric looked at the map and nodded. "What about the south and east?"

"I'll have two small blocking companies in both places. The chances are slim that they will mount an attack from either direction. They won't be able to move through the eastern ridge. And in the south, a narrow road leads to the villa, a sure trap for any vehicles. So, the western approach is probably the direction a mobile reinforcement will make an attempt."

Eric examined the map and nodded in concurrence. "The satellite pictures we got prior to take-off showed an increased activity in this area. It looks like they brought reinforcements to the villa."

"I am sure they did. Kamal is very involved with the Hezbollah movement. His contributions to them don't go unnoticed. I'm sure they'll protect him," Ben said. "Here's what we'll do."

# CHAPTER 23

Kamal nervously paced the bedroom floor, occasionally looking at the tall mountains looming above the villa. Long shadows began to cover the canyons and the rough terrain of the mountain slopes slowly disappeared as evening fell.

"What's causing this delay?" Kamal asked Rashid, his voice rising in anger.

Rashid sat on a sofa facing the window and his face reddened as he spoke. "We have a few complications with the Russians."

"What complications? I paid those bastards more than half their exorbitant demand," Kamal shouted.

"We have a problem with the Iranians as well," Rashid said, his voice low.

Kamal raised his eyes toward the mountains and his lips moved as if in prayer. "The Iranians?"

"Let me explain."

"I have been waiting for an explanation since you got here."

"It's the submarine. The Iranians say they want it for themselves. They've offered the Russians a huge sum for it."

"I don't understand," Kamal said. "You mean the Kilo Class that Pluchenko offered us in Odessa?"

"Yes. Evidently the sales pitch they gave to us impressed Reza Deghani."

"So?"

"They say there is only one submarine of its kind in operation at the present."

"So that son-of-a-bitch convinced the Russians that the Iranian cause is more important!" Kamal banged his fist against the table.

"It's not quite so bad though."

"What do you mean?"

"I made a bargain with both Deghani and Pluchenko. The Iranians will purchase the submarine and will help us transport the team to the US. It will actually save us money."

"A master stroke, indeed," Kamal said and slapped Rashid on the back. "Brilliant. You are to be congratulated."

"There's more. We have the formula as well. That British pharmaceutical executive delivered it to the Iranians and they are all working together—the Russian scientists, the Iranians, and the Brit. It's just a matter of weeks, if not days."

"But how do we get it?"

"It will be brought in from Iraq, through Jordan into the West Bank."

"Past border patrols and custom inspections?"

"No, the smugglers will ford the Jordan River at night and bring it into Jericho in some kind of containers. Legitimate containers that we can deliver to warehouses around the world where the real product in similar packaging is usually distributed. Maybe in olive oil cans or wine casks."

"Our plan is moving ahead," Kamal said, and Rashid noticed relief in his voice.

Kamal turned toward the window to watch the last of the sun's rays fade. When he finally turned toward Rashid, his face glowed triumphantly. "You will be rewarded for all this. You'll be able to retire young."

"Thank you, Ya Rais. I didn't do it just for money, but because I believe in your cause."

The two men embraced and Kamal planted a kiss on each of Rashid's cheeks. "I have a dinner waiting for us in the dining room, specially cooked by my friend, Lila. Come meet her."

"It will be my pleasure," Rashid said, and Kamal pointed the way.

———

Beyond the canyon walls, the contours of the tall dark mountains obscured the sky, and the furrowed granite ridges studded with pine trees glowed in the waning moon.

The commandos crouched, awaiting the signal from the lead scout. After a while, Ben heard the sound of a bird chirp and he motioned to the column to proceed. He sensed that even though they were shrouded in complete darkness, they were very close to the villa.

Mercifully, the canyon's sharp drop leveled off, giving the warriors relief from the heavy loads they carried on their backs that so taxed their knees.

Barely visible under the near dark moon, the villa suddenly came into view at the edge of the canyon. Ben saw the shapes of Eric's men following his movements as they headed west, according to plan.

No talk was permitted. It was a well-conceived operation, Ben thought, and it required silence. His second in command, a young major named Bukki, tapped him on his shoulder, pointing toward the east.

They heard the rumble of heavy vehicles, perhaps tanks moving in the darkness. A Syrian army exercise, Ben thought, as he touched Bukki's hand momentarily, in acknowledgment.

The group split. One column, a blocking force, went east and south. The main force, commanded by Ben, headed straight down the slope toward the villa.

Inside the villa, Kamal tossed restlessly in his bed. With Lila's right breast in one hand and her quiet breathing in his ear, he felt amorous.

He caressed her belly, then the soft hair below it. She moaned and he kissed her passionately. She moved towards him.

He entered her and his strokes sent her cries toward the open window, where two sentries crouched watching the dark mountains.

One of them sneered as the other stood up, unzipping his pants to relieve his bladder. The sound of his urine hitting the basalt rock followed Lila's outcry as she finished, exhausted. Kamal too shuddered, but emitted no sound.

All was quiet then, as the sentries returned to their posts. Savoring his pleasure, Kamal fell into a deep sleep beside Lila.

As the commandos crawled toward the canyon approaches, Ben heard the sound of a metallic object, probably a weapon hitting rock, and he knew that sentries were there waiting. He motioned to four of his commandos and they moved silently ahead, outflanking the direction of the noise. The teams proceeded cautiously toward the villa, their shadows blending with the rugged terrain.

Then they waited. Finally, they heard the cry of a woman. The sound died and Ben suddenly saw the face of a man, his black mustache illuminated by the match he lit. Then darkness engulfed him, and only the glow of his cigarette told the commandos where the next danger lay.

The two sentries fell where they had stood, face down in the dust, and the commandos proceeded toward the main house.

Inside his bedroom, Rashid lay alert. From the window he heard the whisper of the wind in the pines. But then he thought he heard a thud, like a body hitting ground. He froze, listening. Memories of his past with the Egyptian paratroopers and the American commando forces suddenly flooded his mind.

He drew the Glock from atop his night table and released the safety latch. Slowly, he crouched under the window and raised his head to look at the contours of the mountains surrounding the villa. Had it been a good idea to come here? He shrugged off the thought. It was Kamal's idea and Kamal made the decisions.

Rashid raised his head again to peer into darkness illuminated only slightly by the slim edge of moon. He thought he heard another thud. Restless sentries pitching rocks? he wondered.

He could hear Kamal too, talking to his lover in the next room. After a short time, all was quiet again, and Rashid returned to bed.

But he could not fall asleep. He dressed quickly in the dark and tiptoed toward the kitchen, where he hoped to find some of the coffee Lila had prepared earlier, and perhaps some of her delicacies. She was truly a chef extraordinaire, Rashid thought.

He peeked through the kitchen window and saw the shadow of the helicopter he had flown in on, cast against the dark mountains. An uneasy feeling came over him and he decided to alert Kamal and suggest leaving the villa ahead of schedule.

He went toward the bedroom and heard what sounded like breaking glass. He raced toward Kamal's bedroom and opened the door. Kamal stood near the window, his weapon drawn.

"Set the timer," he told Rashid. "Lila get dressed! We're leaving." Kamal pulled out a bag that was always packed and ready from beneath the bed. "We're taking Lila with us," Kamal said firmly.

Rashid did what he was told and set the timer that would give them but a few minutes to get to safety. He saw Lila trembling in the hallway, semi-clad in a bathrobe. "Hurry, Lila! He shouted as he gathered up his things: documents, plans, his cell phone, his own bag. He turned and there she was, frozen in the doorway watching him. He grabbed her hand and pulled her through the house.

Once outside they started across the yard. But suddenly they heard small arms fire come from the direction of the canyon and Lila screamed, pulled away, and ran for cover inside the house. Rashid saw dark figures racing toward them in the shadows.

"I'll get her, once you're safe," he told Kamal, grabbing him by the arm. Rashid yanked him toward the cave and through an opening in the rocks, just before a spectacular blast hit their ears. Within seconds a landslide of earth and boulders sealed off the former entrance to the cave, designed for just such an emergency as a surprise attack.

Neither spoke of Lila or the enemy who had surely been blown up with her; they simply proceeded as planned, in complete silence through a corridor in the mountain.

From the west, Ben heard the sound of helicopters heading their way. These were the birds that would take him and his teams back to the aircraft carrier. His walkie-talkie beeped. "Shamir," he said.

"What the hell happened out there?" the Delta Force commander asked.

"The fucking building blew up right in front of our eyes."

"You sound surprised."

"I am. We didn't do it. And we certainly didn't expect Kamal Ibn-Sultan to destroy his own compound."

"How about your men?"

"Lost some."

"Sorry."

"And the den of thieves?"

"As far as we can tell they blew with the building."

Yes, he was sure of it, even their getaway helicopter had been destroyed. They had killed the enemy and struck at the heart and mind of the terrorist movement.

Leah, my dear, Ben thought, we have avenged your death.

# CHAPTER 24

When Rashid's flight from Montreal landed at JFK, he took a subway to Brooklyn, carrying a large briefcase and one carry-on. He got off at Kings Highway and walked the ten or so blocks to a blighted area of warehouses and abandoned apartment buildings. He stopped at a store next to a boarded-up garage with a rusted-out Pennzoil sign on its door. He went inside and, though he could smell coffee that had been heating too long and cigarette smoke, the place seemed empty. He dinged the little bell on the counter and heard noise in the back room. Ali Bourigiba, the best damn explosive expert Rashid had ever known, came through the door and smiled at him. "Rashid, my old friend," he said and shook his hand.

"Ali Bourigiba, how are you?"

"It's Albert Bourg here."

"Hey, did you do all this? Rashid teased, pointing out the window at the street.

"What? You mean the neighborhood? No, the idiots here did that all by themselves. A few fires, I guess. But, you know, the rent's cheap and no one cares who you are or what you do here."

"Good, because I have a job for you. A very lucrative one."

Bourg went to the door and turned the open sign over to 'closed' and locked it. "Come on back."

Rashid followed him to a room with a cement floor and a couple of old chairs. They sat down.

"Do you still work for that place on Atlantic?" Rashid asked him.

"Yes, and for a couple of others."

"Can you find out who's doing the fireworks for the memorial thing down at the World Trade site in September?"

"Sure, companies put in bids and even submit designs for displays. Why, what do you have in mind?"

Rashid outlined his plan for special fireworks that could be substituted for the real thing at the 9/11 memorial festivities that, he'd just learned from a Palestinian operative, might also celebrate a peace treaty in the Middle East.

"The only problem I can see is making the switch," Bourg said.

"Can it be done?"

"With a little help."

"Good," Rashid said.

When he left Bourg's, Rashid got back on the subway and, at Atlantic Pacific, switched to a train going into Manhattan. He got a cheap hotel near Penn Station and cleaned up. He put on a gray wig, a beret, and a trench coat suitable for this chilly May evening. Then he assembled a collapsible walking stick.

Once on the street, he hailed a cab uptown to Sandra's neighborhood on the east side. When he got out, he limped across the street and then fumbled with the key to the outer door of Sandra's building, like any old man might. Once inside, he went through the second door and to the stairwell next to the elevator. He took off the beret, the wig and the trench coat, collapsed the walking stick, and put it all in the briefcase.

When he got to her floor, he rang her bell and she peeked out. "Well for heaven's sake, come on in," she said, opening the door.

"Sorry I didn't call, but I was closer to your building then to a phone."

"I'm glad I gave you keys. I hope you can stay over," she said, locking

the door behind him. He kissed her and she pulled him across the floor
to her bedroom.

The next morning after Sandra left for work, he sat in the lobby
with a newspaper. When an elderly woman came out of the elevator
with a small dog on a leash, he followed behind her.

"Is that a Pomeranian?" he asked her.

"Why yes," the elderly woman said, pausing at the mailbox.

"Here, let me," he offered. He took the bundle of letters from her
and placed them in the out box. "Aren't you out bright and early?" he
said, smiling.

"Oh, Pepita and I get up at the crack of dawn."

He opened the door for her and walked down the street beside her.
"Pepita looks to be just a couple of years old," he said, holding her arm
to cross at the corner.

"Why, yes," she said, "perhaps you have a Pomeranian yourself."

"No, I've just always liked them."

"They do have personalities," she said and proceeded to explain the
idiosyncrasies of the breed. On the next block, he excused himself and
ducked into a subway entrance.

# CHAPTER 25

Rashid needed a team to board the kilo class submarine and enter the US interior after landing. First, he chose a team commander: former Pakistani rebel leader Massoud El-Tabriz, a man highly recommended by Kamal Ibn-Sultan.

Massoud, who'd been raised by his Afghan father and Pakistani mother in the United States, spoke impeccable English. His father, a successful fruit-merchant on the lower east side of Manhattan, had instilled in him the desire to succeed. His mother had taught him to study, to assimilate information, and to work hard. All that, combined with intelligence, had earned him good grades in school and he'd gone on to Columbia University to study economics.

While still a student, Massoud traveled to Afghanistan to visit his father's family, just before the Soviet invasion. By the time the Afghan rebels' fight against the Russian army had intensified, he'd met Kamal Ibn-Sultan, who convinced him to fight alongside him. Later, when the Taliban came to power, Massoud became one of their young leaders under his sponsorship.

After a visit to a Hezbollah training camp in the Bekaa valley, Rashid traveled to Syria. He asked Massoud to meet him for dinner at a small restaurant in the heart of the Damascus marketplace, the Suk, as the locals called it, to decide on another four team members.

After they finished a dinner of grilled fish, shish kebab, humus and tahina, the proprietor whispered something in Rashid's ear.

"Come," Rashid said to Massoud, "Our host has provided us with a private room where we can talk undisturbed."

Massoud followed Rashid into a room lit by a kerosene lamp and they sat down on sofas facing each other. The proprietor brought them some black, sweet coffee laced with a hint of hale the way Rashid liked it, and two nargilah water pipes. The men filled the pipes and settled in to choose team members from among the volunteers who'd aided the Afghan rebels in their fight against the Russian army.

One of these was Hans Kruger, a former German Red Brigade member. Another was Nadia Tlass, a former PLO terrorist who'd participated in the famous high-jacking of a Sabena Airlines aircraft in Athens during the hey-day of terrorist activities.

A third member was Aldo Gardini, a Sicilian whose mother was an Afghan. After his mother died of cancer, he lived with his father in Montallegro and grew up there. After college, he went to Afghanistan. Impressed by Afghan rebels related to his mother and their associate, Kamal Ibn-Sultan, he joined them.

The last team member they chose was Sammy Hupy, born to a black American soldier and a Vietnamese mother during the Vietnam War. Sammy grew up in Brooklyn after his father brought him and his mother to the States when the war ended.

Later, after graduating from high school, Sammy and his mother went back to Vietnam for a visit. He befriended his mother's cousin, who persuaded Sammy to join him as a volunteer in the Afghan rebel army. The cousin told Sammy about an interesting man he'd met in Afghanistan, one of the rising leaders of the rebels named Kamal Ibn-Sultan. Sammy's curiosity prevailed and, after meeting Ibn-Sultan, was convinced his cause was right. He stayed and fought alongside him in many of the battles against the Russians.

"So, we have our team, all good people loyal to our cause," Rashid told Massoud once they were done.

"Have you chosen a date for our departure?" Massoud asked.

"No, but soon, so start training your team as if in real combat on American soil. I've arranged for you to take them to the Hezbollah training camp in the Bekaa Valley of Lebanon. After that your team will travel separately, first to Moscow, then by train to St. Petersburg where they are to wait for you. You and I will meet in Vienna at that Turkish coffee house by the Danube River where we met last time. After our meeting, you'll fly directly to St. Petersburg."

Massoud nodded.

"Your papers and your team's will all be in order. Meanwhile Kamal is working on the final details. I'll let you know when I have them."

"We will be waiting," Massoud said.

"Good, the kilo class sub from Odessa will precede us."

Rashid smiled, got up, and went to the window. He pulled the curtain aside and peeked into the teeming Suk. "Then, when I contact you, you will proceed with the plan. So, carry your cell phone at all times."

"What code will you use?"

'Shah-Mut,' or as the westerners say, 'Checkmate.'"

"A good name. The end-game, the game of all games," Massoud said.

Rashid nodded. They stood in silence, watching the flame of the kerosene lamp flicker. He thought of a time on the Cayman Islands with Sandra. They had stood on the balcony of her hotel suite very late one night looking out at a life-sized chess set in the magnificent garden below. "A giant chess set?" he'd asked her, puzzled.

"Yes," Sandra had explained. "It's a game based on real chess and it requires you to keep one step ahead of your opponent in order to capture his holdings. It's even called 'Checkmate.'"

How appropriate, he had thought. Just like life. Turning to Massoud, he looked at his watch. "It's time to leave," he told him.

"Send Kamal my greetings," Massoud said. "Tell him that we are all behind him."

The two hugged and Massoud kissed him on each cheek and bade him good-by.

# CHAPTER 26

It was a gray, rainy morning and Sandra had to turn on the light over her desk, though it was in front of the window. She began to systematically organize the clutter of mail, separating the throwaway from the unpaid bills that had been there for weeks.

There was a large Manila envelope at the bottom of a pile of letters and catalogues she'd put there the night before, after getting home late. The return address was smeared, as if the package had gotten caught in the rain. She opened it anyway, and took out a thick typed report from a trusted associate who worked at her company's London office. She read the note attached: "Sandra, take a look. The modified anthrax formula, and maybe a whole lot more, appears to have been given or sold to some Iranian agent by Lloyd Jeoffreys, VP at A.C. Hitchcock. Remember him? Evidently, he hooked up with former Russian scientists involved in germ warfare and sold out for who knows how much. Scary stuff. Give me a call, Laura."

John Devine called Roger at home early to say he would be by to pick him up. Roger was in the lobby waiting for him when the limo pulled up at the curb in front of his apartment building. It was raining hard and sheaths of it covered the lobby window, making the morning light as dim as dusk. Roger had not brought an umbrella and he darted around several puddles to the car and got into the back seat.

He wiped water from his face and smiled at Devine. "So, what's the occasion?"

"We're making a house calls today. Sandra Savino."

"Yeah? Business or pleasure?"

"Here's the deal. Airport security in Montreal got a random photo of someone who looks suspiciously like your favorite terrorist, who we thought had become Lebanese topsoil. This look-alike flew into JFK and that's all we know."

"Damn, that would mean the kilo sub plot is not going away."

"Yeah, so I think it's time we confront the beautiful scientist with some photos."

"So why at her home?"

"Because surveillance says that's where she is today. Of course, I wasted half an hour trying to track her down at her office before thinking to ask them."

Roger laughed. "Surveillance hasn't noticed anything unusual since the attack on Ibn-Sultan's compound, have they?"

"No, and no activity on her phone either. But we don't have taps inside, do we?"

"No. Maybe we should install some."

The limo stopped in front of a large building and John Devine got on the car phone and dialed a number.

"Ms. Savino," he said, "This is John Devine. I think you've met my associate Roger Shaw. Yes. Well, we'd like to talk to you for a few minutes." Devine winked at Roger. "Now would be good. We're just outside your apartment building. Would you buzz us in? . . . Okay, we'll watch for you."

When Sandra appeared at the door of the building, the two got out and hurried through the downpour to the awning. She held the door for them and they followed her through a second door to the lobby and elevator. John Devine introduced himself and shook her hand. "And you remember Roger, do you not?"

"I do," she said and graciously shook his hand also.

They got on the elevator and the three were silent. The door opened and they followed her to her door. She unlocked it and ushered them in, then seated them in the living room, adjacent to a large window. The rain outside had become torrential and gusts of wind from the East River threw sudden sheets of it noisily against the glass, obscuring the view of the river completely.

"Ms. Savino," Devine said. "Take a look at these photos. Do they look like anyone you know?"

Sandra looked at them curiously. "I don't know. This one looks like a stereotypical picture of a terrorist, you know, the beard, the camouflage, the hat and gun."

"How about the other one?"

"This one resembles a friend of mine. But it's too grainy to tell. Why?"

"One we know to be a known terrorist, Rashid Al-Sharif, the other may be him."

"But I thought he and that Ibn-Sultan were blown up in an explosion in Afghanistan or somewhere a few weeks ago."

"Lebanon. But we're not sure. The second picture was taken since that explosion at the airport in Montreal. The one of the man you say looks like your friend."

Sandra frowned.

"Tell us about him."

"His name is Ray Cohn. I don't see him too often because he lives abroad. He deals in imports from all over the world. I've known him for several years."

"When did you see him last?"

"About ten days ago. He stayed overnight here."

Roger and John both looked at each other in surprise.

"Could you tell us exactly when?"

Sandra got up and went to her desk and flipped through a day planner. "May 12th."

"Okay, we'll find out when the photo was taken. But we have to caution you. If your Ray is Rashid Al-Sharif, it doesn't look good for you—for a scientist of your caliber to be associated with a known terrorist, who deals in the exact product your company produces."

"Excuse me. My company does not produce germ warfare. As I explained to Mr. Shaw in an earlier conversation, we are scientists who are for life, not against it. And if my friend looks like a dead man you should have gotten alive, and you start harassing him, then it doesn't look good for you either, Mr. Devine."

Sandra Savino got up, making it clear that they were no longer welcome. "Is there any more questions, gentlemen?"

Both men stood up. "Yes, you've heard of Lloyd Jeoffreys, haven't you?" Devine asked.

"Of course."

"We have disturbing information about him, too."

Again, she went to her desk. "This, you mean?" She handed him the report with the attached note.

Devine scanned it and handed it to Roger. "Who is this from?"

"One of my associates in London. I just opened it. I haven't read the report yet."

"Hmmm," Devine said. "Frankly Ms. Savino, we need your help."

"How?"

"We know that your company was conducting research that parallels what your British competitors were doing. We need to know exactly what Jeoffreys sold to the Iranians. So, if you'd be willing to meet with someone from our office and see if you, and perhaps people you work with, could make some educated guesses, you know, about what he sold and the harm it might do. That sort of thing."

"You can send someone over to my office this afternoon. Or come yourself."

"Will do," Devine said. "Then there's the Al-Sharif thing. If your friend Ray contacts you at any time, day or night, I'd like to be informed."

Sandra frowned at him.

"I just want to talk to him. If he's just this look-alike, we should know, especially if he travels abroad. You don't want some other government mistaking him for a terrorist, do you?"

"Of course not. But, remember Al-Sharif was killed in an explosion."

Devine ignored her comment. "And I'd like to send someone over to check for fingerprints."

Sandra went a third time to her desk. "Fine," she said, looking through a drawer. She sorted through some photos. "Here. This is Ray Cohn," she said and handed him one from the stack.

"Can we take this?"

"Yes, but I want it back when you're done with it."

"Certainly. And if your friend checks out, I'll send over some Dom Perignon for your next get together."

"I'll look forward to that."

He handed her a card. "My private line." She took it and shut the door behind them.

By the time they got down to the street, the rain had let up. Back in the limo, Roger studied the picture. "This guy does look good in Speedos."

"Is it Al-Sharif?"

"I don't know for sure. Certainly, there's a resemblance. But this is so out of context. It looks like an ad from Gentlemen's Quarterly."

Devine got on the phone again. "Send someone in to Savino's to check for fingerprints, and anything else. And while you're at it, install some listening equipment. Get on it though, before she leaves. Oh, yeah, and send me over any photo shoots from the past several weeks; you guys missed an overnighter." He hung up.

"That to me is a huge flag," Roger said.

"What?"

"A normal visitor would have been spotted."

"Yeah, but this one should have been too."

"So, who's going to Savino's office?"

"How about Linda? She's a scientist, isn't she?"

"Yes, a biologist. And maybe Savino will like her better than us."

John Devine laughed. "See what she thinks of these pictures. She's the only one of us who knows what the bastard looks like." His phone buzzed and he picked it up. "Devine".

"Uh-huh. Got it." He hung up and whistled.

"What?" Roger asked.

"The Iranians haven't killed Jeoffreys yet, apparently they're putting him to work. He visited an area outside Moscow, where Viktor Shalyapin was once developing deadly viruses for the Soviets. Shalyapin was his tour guide." He paused, looking at Roger.

"Also, frantic activity at the Odessa dry dock where a Kilo Class sub is going through an extensive overhaul—including a visitor. Reza Deghani."

"That fucking Iranian is getting to be a regular there. You think the Iranians are putting in a bid in for the sub?"

"I don't know, but I want you to find out where it's going before it hits any waves."

# CHAPTER 27

Linda looked at the photos and handed them back to Roger. "I can't tell. Why don't these security people invest in some good camera equipment? You can get clearer pictures at one of those booths at the mall." She got up. "You want half my sandwich?"

"No, thanks. But I would drink some of that coffee you made."

Linda brought over cups from a counter adjacent to her desk and poured them both some coffee."

"Devine wants you to go over to Sandra's office and get the skinny on whatever Jeoffrey's might have sold the bad guys."

Linda sat down at her desk and bit her lip in silence.

"Your wheels are spinning. What's going on?"

"I was just thinking. What if I meet with that Russian scientist who approached Sandra and . . ."

"Oh, no. Absolutely not. Don't even think about it!"

"Why not? You think they're not going to see through a CIA operative who's never even looked through a microscope? You need someone closer to the scientific community here."

"Fine, but that someone is not going to be you!"

"Roger, listen to yourself. You're acting pretty parental here. You can't forbid this!"

"As your boss I certainly can."

"Don't you dare pull rank on me, because we're sleeping together."

Roger got up and paced back and forth in front of her desk silently. "Say something."

"I'm too pissed off."

"All I want to do is talk to him. Or maybe to someone connected to that Russian sub. Maybe I could build a case for wanting some drugs transported from one seaport to another across the world. Or at least I could see if the sub is still there without even mentioning it. Maybe I could just be a tourist or a journalist. Surely, the Russians have a legitimate navy spokesperson I could talk to."

Roger sighed and pulled out her office chair and kneeled down in front of her.

"I'm not trying to pull rank or forbid you from anything, I just want you safe. If something should happen to you, I don't think I could bear it."

"But something did happen to Leah and I want to do this for her. Please, Roger, please. Eric can go with me. You can be on the sidelines. I promise, I'll be careful. I'm not going to do anything to endanger the information I want to get."

"Don't ask me, Linda. Don't!"

Linda got up. "Okay, I'll ask John Devine." She grabbed her jacket from the closet and headed toward the door.

"He'll say no, too," Roger said, following her out the door.

———

"You know, it could work," John Devine told Roger. "We could provide her with the credentials, a cover, whatever it takes. She could even interview Vice Admiral Yevgeny Katuzov."

"No, I'll interview him."

"Then she could talk to Shalyapin."

"Oh, my god, what have I done?"

"What do you mean?"

"To think I recruited her."

"Roger, have you gotten emotionally involved with Linda?"

"Christ almighty, yes."

"She can't work under you anymore."

"I know, I know. I don't want her to work under anyone. I want her to go back to Harvard and work with Mark!"

"Roger, you're forgetting one thing."

"What?"

"It's her life."

"I got to get some air."

"She'll be fine," Devine hollered after him, but Roger was already out the door.

———

A secretary took Linda to Sandra Savino's office door and knocked. "Ms. Ashcroft to see you."

"Come in," Sandra Savino said from her desk.

"Sit down, Ms. Ashcroft."

"Linda. Will do."

"Okay, Linda, I understand you need some information."

"Yes, but more than John Devine thought when he spoke to you. I need to sound credible in front of that Russian scientist who contacted you."

"Victor Shalyapin?"

"Yes. I need to convince him that I'm your assistant who's selling whatever he wanted from you and that I might have something that Jeoffreys doesn't have. And that I was in contact with Rashid Al-Sharif before his supposed death."

"Were you?"

"Yes."

"Do you think Al-Sharif is dead?"

"I don't know, but I want to find out."

"I don't get it. You sound like an intelligent woman. Yet, I hear these terrorists are dangerous. I heard that from the very guys who sent you, in fact. Why risk your life to do something one of these gung-ho CIA types are trained to do?"

Linda didn't say anything for a moment. When she did speak, her voice was quiet, even. "My best friend was a scientist like you. She was one of those beings who lived her life under one rule. That rule was: do no harm. She wouldn't have violated the corpse of a dead frog if she didn't think it would advance the well-being of a living one. And, because of people like Rashid Al-Sharif who believe they know what's right for the world and then kill anybody who doesn't agree—because of people like that—my friend is dead. So, I want to know the truth here, don't you?"

Sandra Savino sighed. "Yes. Let's get to work." She got up and pulled the file on Verdat Industries and Victor Shalyapin.

# CHAPTER 28

———

The article in *The New York Times* caught John Devine's eye as he
sat down with Chinese take-out Sunday afternoon in his Langley
office: "Plans for the September 11th memorial ceremony, on the site
where the World Trade Center buildings and five others once stood,
have been finalized. The ceremony will include the Israeli premier and
newly elected Palestinian authority chairman. The two dignitaries are
scheduled to sign a landmark peace treaty between their nations the
following day at the UN. The treaty will make Palestine an independent
state and, world leaders hope, bring an end to violence in the Middle
East."

Well, that sure as hell raises the ante, Devine thought. A situation
already a natural target for terrorism has now been made a thousand
times sweeter.

His fax machine started up and he grabbed the message coming out
of the printer. It was from his deputy: "John, we have the Israeli Mossad
estimates of Russian experts assisting Iran's biological, chemical, and
nuclear weapons programs. They say Iran has up to 10,000 Russian
experts helping them with special projects—one of those the biologist,
Dr. Valery Bakayev, who worked at the Pasteva Institute in Teheran
for more than five years, supposedly on the development of vaccines.
The Israelis estimate a hundred or so other experts are helping Iran
develop the Shihab-3 and Shihab-4 ballistic missiles, as well as a missile

identified as the SS-400, known to have a range of 3,600 kilometers. These missiles could be in operation by the year 2004, and capable of carrying nuclear warheads by 2007. What the other 9,899 other Russian experts are doing, they didn't say. Let's get together on this soon. Gordon."

Devine sighed and looked at his e-mail screen. A new coded message was coming through with Roger's signature on it. He opened it: "Kilo class sub no longer in Odessa, but a look-alike spotted at Admiralty Shipyard in St. Petersburg. Request permission to proceed to that location."

"Son-of a bitch," Devine said aloud. He typed in an answer: *Check it out, but don't you go near that operation with Eric and Linda. Repeat. Don't go near her! You'll put her in danger!* Then he added: *I will keep you appraised, I promise.*

Devine started an answer to his deputy, but he couldn't concentrate. "Damn!" he said aloud and buzzed his assistant. Within a minute he entered. "Sir?" he said.

"Carl, I know you're headed for a family barbecue, but Roger Shaw's going to be right in the middle of that thing in St. Pete with Eric LaGrange and Linda Ashcroft. Send in some backup before you go."

"But sir, with all due respect—Roger's as level headed as they come. What makes you think he'll go off half-cocked?"

"Because in the same position, I would. And get me Aaron Golan on the phone too."

"Of course, Sir," he said and closed the door behind him.

Within minutes, Devine's phone rang and he picked it up. "Devine here."

"Yes, Aaron. We got a situation here. I need your help."

———

The passenger in the first-class section of British Air Flight 230 to St. Petersburg shifted her gaze to her row mate, an elderly man wearing fashionable round reading glasses, perched on his crooked nose. The seat between them was empty. Linda put on her earphones and lay back, trying to concentrate on the interview ahead. She tried to relax and project herself into the hours to come, visualizing herself poised, self-confident and unafraid—in spite of being scared to death.

Linda put her seat upright as the aircraft made its descent. When they heard the landing gear open, the elderly man looked at his watch and shook his head. "It looks like we're late."

Great, she thought. The craft taxied toward the gate and when it finally stopped, she collected her bag and inched toward the exit.

Outside she saw a driver holding up a sign with her name misspelled: L. Ashcraft. She was also aware of Eric nearby, waiting for another cab. They did not make eye contact.

When she got to Verdat Industries, an abandoned looking grouping of buildings, the driver told her he'd wait for her. Inside the main one, she was surprised to find its interior quite nice. Apparently, more business went on here than the world knew about after all. Another man held up a sign with her name, also misspelled. He showed her to Mr. Shalyapin's office and he appeared to be waiting too. It was positively eerie.

"I'm sorry I'm late," she said and shook his hand.

"Yes, I checked. Your plane was behind schedule. Before we begin, I'm sure you don't mind if we do a wire search?"

"No, of course not, as long as a woman does it."

"Please, this way," he said and opened a door for her.

Once the body search was over, Linda was led back into the same office. She took the seat Shalyapin pointed to.

"I was surprised to hear from someone from the Laguna Corporation," he said. "Sandra Savino certainly didn't seem too interested."

"Oh, but she didn't speak for all of us."

"I see. So, what can I do for you?"

"According to your file at Laguna, you were interested in a merger."

"I was. But I have since made other arrangements."

"Yes, with Lloyd Jeoffreys."

"And how do you know that?"

"Rashid told me."

"Rashid Al-Sharif?"

"Yes, when I met with him in Istanbul. But of course, everyone at A. C. Hitchcock and the rest of the world knows of Jeoffrey's defection by now."

"When was that meeting with Rashid?"

"Certainly, before his recent accident."

"Exactly?"

"I believe it was early January."

"Hmmm, so there were better reasons than just sex for Mr. Al-Sharif's hands-off thing with Miss Savino. Maybe he draws from two decks."

"No doubt. Anyway, as far as I can tell from my research, the Hitchcock group does not have an antidote that will work after exposure to even the slightest variation in temperature. Certainly, it won't work out in the field."

"And you have one that does?"

"Let's just say, I will. I have access not only to the work at Laguna, but also to what the Harvard team is doing in Boston. You see, I studied under Mark Lindsey, who's head of that research."

"So, Miss Ashcroft, why would you do business with us? I find that most scientists aren't as interested in money as I am."

"Here's the deal. I'm comfortable giving you the antidote. The poison itself would keep me up nights. However, I want you to make it appear to have come from Ms. Savino. Simply put, I want her job."

"I see. And if you work for us, can you guarantee you won't also be dealing with Mr. Al-Sharif?"

"How could I now? He's supposed to be dead."

"And you believe that?"

"It was in all the papers."

"You Americans. You always take anything in print for truth."

"So, you don't think so?"

"Let me put it this way. If you elect to work with us and you're caught associating with him, you will be the one dead and in all the papers."

"Well put. Do we have a tentative deal?"

"Yes. Of course, I have to check you out, you understand."

"Perfectly. Meanwhile I will compile the data and I trust you will get back to me." She handed him her card.

"Definitely," he said and shook her hand again.

When Linda had gone, Shalyapin opened a second door off his office. "Did you get all that?"

"Yes."

"Who is she?"

"I don't know."

"Either she's trying to put one over on us and sell us something Rashid doesn't want—or already has—or she's selling to both of us. But she's right about that temperature variation problem."

"What troubles me is that she thinks Rashid's dead."

"Or maybe she knows he's not and wonders what we know."

"Maybe it's that she's already sold to him and he hasn't let her know he's still around to pay off."

"Yeah, something like that. Perhaps he's going to pitch us the same deal with a big markup. Try to get another Kilo sub deal."

"There certainly will be people interested in knowing that Al-Sharif met with a scientist on the side."

"Or with someone posing as one."

"I don't trust Al-Sharif or anyone who's ever worked for the CIA."

"Maybe Kamal Ibn-Sultan doesn't either."

"What are you saying?"

"Let's see if he knows about his lieutenant's meeting with a Miss Ashcroft."

Once back in the car, Linda let out a sigh of relief. "The airport please." The driver didn't answer and she looked at the back of his head and leaned forward. "You're not the same driver."

"No, his shift is over."

"Oh," she said, suddenly on guard. "This isn't the way we came in."

"No, the traffic will be better this way."

She looked out the back window. There wasn't any traffic, except for a car behind them. When they turned left at a T in the road, she looked back to see the car behind them turn left too. Where the hell was Eric? She wondered.

# CHAPTER 29

"I can only get so close to the shipyard by car," the driver of the old Bentley said to his passenger.

Roger nodded and held his briefcase, watching the scenery of the St. Petersburg waterfront pass by the window of the vehicle. They were approaching an isolated spot between the quay and the Admiralty Shipyard gate. Roger took out a pair of powerful binoculars and scanned the distant shipyard. He discerned the outline of what appeared to be a submarine in dry dock.

"Those are deadly submarines," the driver said. "Quite a few rogue nations are interested in acquiring them."

"From what you told me, Ivan, I can see why. How close is the shipyard to the gate?"

"It's about half a mile off the road," Ivan said. "You won't see much on the way to your appointment."

Roger sat quietly, deep in thought, staring out the vehicle's window. "How good is the security at the shipyard?"

"It's spotty, because of budget problems. You know about the bleak state of our economy," Ivan replied.

Roger nodded, looking toward the shipyard. "Any special forces here to your knowledge?"

"Yes, but their numbers have dwindled in recent months, again due to lack of funds. Some of their soldiers have to moon-light as waiters or the like to supplement their income."

"A sad state. Still, if they're the best you have, they are undoubtedly here at the shipyard."

"Probably." Ivan looked at Roger, waiting for the next step.

"All right then," Roger said, "Try to get a good look while I'm inside. Get as many details as you can."

"I'll make the shipyard crew think I'm bored and curious."

Roger noticed Ivan's jaws tighten. He leaned over to the glove compartment and took out a flask of vodka. He offered it to Roger. "For luck?"

"Why not," Roger said, and they both took a swig.

"I'll just wander around," Ivan said and smiled. He held up the flask and tapped on its lid, indicating that it held a tiny camera.

"As soon as you have all you can get, call my beeper."

Ivan nodded and started the engine, and the Bentley moved slowly toward the shipyard gate.

The Russian fleet commander, Vice Admiral Yevgeny Katuzov was older than Roger expected, a leathery faced man who might have stood too many watches on deck in a gale.

"Mr. Shaw, welcome to Russia. May I extend my sympathies for all your country has been through from terrorism these last several years. Unfortunately, what was once a regional problem is now all over the globe."

"Yes, I'm afraid so. What I wanted to talk to you about is your Kilo 636 submarines. We're afraid the terrorists have one of them."

"I've heard that rumor too, but it's false. We don't even have one operating ourselves, though we've been working on the kilos for years. Frankly, there are problems. We had one sink on its sea trial just recently. It will be some time before we recover it and figure out the flaw, I'm afraid. Corruption is rampant, more so than ever before. I can't even show you around, as I would like, as we're somewhat at a standstill. As you can see, there are no longer any Kilo class subs here but those two in dry-dock. But I would like to offer you some food and drink and perhaps a tour of the city. The old palace, perhaps, and the magnificent Neva waterfront?"

Roger had to stall. "Thank you, but first, I would like to use the facilities if I could. It's been a long day with no stops."

"Of course. I'll show you the way."

Roger used the urinal in a bathroom that, like the Vice Admiral, had seen better days and returned to his host's office.

"Now for some repast," the Russian commander said, pointing to a tray of Vodka, bread and caviar.

Thank god, his beeper went off. "Excuse me," Roger said and turned it off. "I'm afraid this means I have to go. Apparently, I'm headed back to the States. But thank you for agreeing to see me on such short notice." He shook the commander's hand and exited.

'Next stop, find Linda,' he thought. He got into the car and neither he nor Ivan spoke, assuming that while both were out of the Bentley, a bug had been placed inside. Ivan did give him the high sign, however, to let him know he'd been successful. There was something repulsive about the Vice Admiral, Roger thought. He was lying through his teeth about the kilo sinking, for one thing.

As soon as they were out of sight of the shipyard and its gate, Ivan said, "Excuse me, Mr. Shaw. I would like to stop to pee."

"Of course," Roger answered. As soon as they pulled over, they both got out. Once out of earshot of the car, Roger got on his phone. "Eric, what have you got?"

"Linda's in a car going toward the city."

"She's supposed to return directly back to the airport."

"I know. Also, there's some tails, in fact, a parade of them. It's spooky."

"Okay, give me your location and we'll get in line, I guess." Frankly, Roger was worried, extremely so.

# CHAPTER 30

They were headed toward a commercial area of the city as far as Linda could tell. Soon they were into heavy traffic as the roadway narrowed down to two lanes. She leaned over the front seat. "If Dostoyevsky could only see the place now," she said. The driver did not respond. "Does this road go by the old palace?" she asked. "No," the driver said. She was silent for a few minutes then asked. "Can you recommend a good tour?"

"No," he said again.

"I was just reading that it takes eleven hours for the sun to pass from Cape Dezhnev to the Gulf of Finland. Do you believe it? Why not? Russia is larger than South America. But you probably knew that." The driver was silent and evidently annoyed. He honked at other drivers and cursed under his breath.

"My grandmother on my father's side came from the Ukraine when she was a young girl. I think she traveled to Finland first then went across the Atlantic. She was probably one of those people to be in quarantine or whatever they did on Ellis Island. Or was it Roosevelt Island? But they probably didn't call any island Roosevelt, then. And when they decided to, I think they named it after Theodore, not Franklin Delano. What do you think? But you probably wouldn't know, would you?"

The driver swerved between two cars and honked. They were coming up to a traffic jam and cars were stopped for at least a couple dozen **car**-lengths in the heart of an area of small shops and open markets. "Sorry, maybe you don't understand conversational English very well," she said as he lurched to a stop behind the jam of cars in front of them.

"No, lady!" he shouted.

She had irritated him sufficiently, she thought, as she got out. "I'll go find a driver who does," she said and slammed the door. She ran down the street and turned back to see the driver chasing after her. She ducked into a crowd of people shopping in an area of kiosks and wooden booths. She thought she had lost him and slowed down to get around a dozen of people waiting in line at a bakery. Suddenly the driver appeared out of nowhere and grabbed her around the neck. The crowd opened up and she ducked under his arm, turned and kneed him between the legs. He cried out, let go, and grabbed his testicles. The crowd went, Oooh!, and Linda continued running and, suddenly, an arm pulled her into a doorway. She yanked free and turned. "Roger!"

"Hi, there," he said and pulled her inside a door. Once the door closed, he fumbled with the lock. "Darn, I guess we broke that. Over here," he said and pulled her through the dark. They crouched down behind a stack of something she couldn't make out.

"I'll bet that guy will think twice before trying to choke any more ladies."

"You saw that?"

"I did. Martial arts, huh?"

"Nope."

"Then where did you learn it?"

"The housemother in my college dorm taught us, so we could walk safely across campus after dark."

"Lord, but this place stinks. Ivan are you still here?"

"Above you."

The two looked up at a man peeking over a tarp spread across the rafters. "Linda, meet Ivan."

Just then someone burst through the door and lights went on. The two froze from their hiding spot behind a six-foot stack of animal pelts. They were evidently in the storage area of a leather tanning shop. Two men with revolvers stood at the open door and a third moved towards them.

"Linda, where are you?" a voice called out. Linda peered from behind the pile of what appeared to be ermine. "Ben Shamir?" she asked. She got up and the two embraced. "Are you doing okay?"

"I've been better."

"You know how much Leah loved you," she said, wiping away tears.

"I know."

"What are you doing here?"

"Leah's father sent me, he said you might need help."

"How is Aaron?"

"He's having a hard time too. How about you?"

"I am hanging in there," she said and kissed his cheek.

Roger coughed behind them. "You just happened to be in the neighborhood?"

"Oh, Ben, this is Roger Shaw."

"Ah, the famous Roger Shaw," he said and the two shook hands. "As a matter of fact, we're here tracking down a rumor that a certain sub sank."

"Did it?"

"Nope, and it's long gone."

"Don't shoot, I'm coming down," Ivan yelled from the rafters. "And that's Ivan," Roger said pointing to Ivan as he swung from one of the open beams to the ground.

"Hello," Ben said. "Let's get the hell out of here, shall we?"

# CHAPTER 31

Music was coming from the street as Rashid sat sipping black Turkish coffee with Massoud on the verandah of a cafe overlooking the Danube. It was a piano concerto that Sandra had often played for him at her New York apartment. It occurred to him that he still missed her every day. His loins ached for her touch, but he couldn't see her again. It had become too late for them, he knew that. But he couldn't help thinking about her and wondering where she was and what she was doing.

A freighter came into view on the Danube and the two men watched it go by. "There's been a change in our plans," Rashid told Massoud. "I have to split up your team."

"You're taking someone with you?"

"No, Aldo Gardini and Nadia Tlass have been reassigned to another task. Kamal met with some of his senior security people last week and they came up with an interesting idea."

"What idea?"

"Aldo and Nadia will penetrate Israeli security. And they'll coordinate their arrival there with our landing in the U.S."

"An ambitious plan."

"Yes, but you and what's left of your team will have to proceed as planned.

"With so little manpower?"

"Don't worry. Everything will work out and I will join you in New York to help. And I am adding another man to your team. Enrique Mondano, an Amazon Indian. He is a very sophisticated warrior, indeed. An expert dart blower."

"And that will help us, the dart blowing?"

"Definitely," Rashid said, pausing to sip his coffee and watch the large barge loaded with iron ore moving slowly downstream. "His little pipe can go where other weapons can't."

"But is it as effective?"

"Oh, yes. I once saw him kill a gazelle on the run with a small poisoned dart. The man has powerful lungs."

"A gazelle?"

"Yes, in the Amazon Basin when I served with the Special Forces in the American army."

The Delta Force had been training in the Brazilian jungle and Rashid had been sent ahead of the commandos to look for a campsite. And there was Enrique, a rugged, tall Indian with jet-black hair, his face covered with red dust, yelling at a dozen other Indians clearing the tall trees lining the river bank. He had a deep, strong voice and spoke to his fellow tribesmen with authority. Rashid had smiled at him and offered him an American cigarette.

A month later while still on maneuvers in the Amazon, the unit came upon a loggers' camp, and there he was again. Here, Rashid saw Enrique's real talent as a jungle scout and his unique skill at dart blowing.

"So, when will this man join us?" Massoud asked.

"When you get to the Admiralty in St. Petersburg. He will fly there directly from Rio. I think he'll work well with Hans and Sammy. Good men, all of them. Has your team completed training?"

"Yes, everyone is ready," Massoud assured him.

"How did they take the hardship?"

"They endured it with dignity, I must say. The woman Nadia did especially well. She is a tough lady and very good with explosives."

"Yes," Rashid said, "She has pulled quite a few daredevil acts on her own. She was involved in that attack on an aircraft in Athens a few years ago. That's why the 'Rais' wanted her on the team heading for Israel."

"I see one possible problem though. Hans' heavy accent could become a problem when we get to New York."

"I don't think it's going to handicap us any, but watch how it goes when you get there. I give you full authority to deal with it in my absence."

"Sometimes, I look at you with wonder," Massoud said. "The way you pull everybody and everything together."

Rashid nodded and stood up. "There is much work ahead of us. You're returning to the training camp?"

"Yes," Massoud said, getting up too. He put a black fedora on his head that complemented the dark striped business suit he'd worn for the occasion. He extended his hand to Rashid, who shook it warmly. "Be careful at the airport," Rashid told him. "You're an irreplaceable leader." They hugged each other and Massoud left.

Rashid watched him as he walked quickly toward a taxi stand waving to a driver. After the taxi and its passenger drove away, Rashid faced the Danube and its fast current. Sandra's face came to him again and she was calling his name.

# CHAPTER 32

The priest wearing a wide-brimmed black hat looked at the long line of nuns waiting to board the El-Al flight from Bergamo to Tel-Aviv. His keen eyes discerned one in particular, a nun with olive-black eyes that complemented her white headpiece. Her thick eyebrows arched when she spotted two Israeli security men mingling with the other passengers.

The two security men appeared to move through the crowded airport with ease, but the priest knew that they were dutifully vigilant. He walked calmly by them, toward the men's room located at the end of the hallway.

Once inside, he examined his face and attire in the mirror. Satisfied with what he saw, he went into a stall and took out his passport. He liked the new name. He was Father Giovanni Santini, a parish priest from Genoa on his way to the holy land to visit Jerusalem and other Christian landmarks, including the site at Capernaum where Jesus had preached. The forger of the passport had done an excellent job indeed.

He tucked the passport inside his wide black coat, left the stall, and glanced one last time at the mirror to examine his appearance. He now sported a month-old black beard and his gray eyes looked black from the tinted lenses that his contact in the safe house in Milan had given him. Not only had his contact provided the lenses, but also documents, the passport, and a place on the tour group's itinerary as a paid-in-full customer.

Time to head back, Aldo realized when he heard the announcement on the airport intercom that El-Al Flight 005 was ready for boarding. He exited the men's room and saw one of the Israeli security men walking along the long line of pilgrims at the boarding gate. He knew that each of the passengers would be interrogated and personally searched by El-Al security personnel.

It had been a good idea to leave the gun in the apartment in Milan, Aldo thought, as he joined the others in line to await his turn. From the corner of his eye, he caught sight of the nun again. An El-Al security woman was talking to her and she appeared to Aldo to exude calmness, though she fingered the beads in her hand as she answered the guard's questions.

Soon, another security woman joined the first and began frisking the nun, whose facial expression did not change. Aldo noticed that her dark eyebrows arched again when she recognized him standing in line.

"What brings you to the holy land, Father?" an El-Al security woman asked him.

"I am going to visit our holy places," Aldo said in an even voice, trying to make his accent sound Italian and not Sicilian.

"You are part of this group?"

"Yes, of course."

"May I see your passport, please?"

Aldo dipped into his wide coat pocket, brought out the document, and handed it to her. She took her time comparing the bearded face in front of her to the one in the passport, then asked Aldo to step aside. She began talking rapidly to a black button in her lapel in a language he suspected was Hebrew.

The security agent went on to another priest, then suddenly turned back to Aldo, surprising him. "Did you pack your luggage yourself or did someone help you?"

"I did all of the packing."

"Do you have anyone waiting for you in Israel? Did you make any arrangements for a tour guide?"

It was annoying how she kept asking two questions at once. "As I said, I am with the tour here and our guide has arranged everything," Aldo said, looking her straight in the eyes.

Suddenly, two security men materialized out of nowhere and stood on each side of Aldo. "Please come with us, Father. It's a routine check," one of the men said, leading the way to a makeshift booth.

Once inside, Aldo found himself facing a third man. He was tall and muscular and his blond hair was trimmed crew-cut style, reminding Aldo of his college days at the university in Bologna.

You are Father Santini, yes?" the blond security man asked.

Aldo nodded and the man examined his passport.

"You're from Genoa?"

"Yes."

"Have you ever been to the holy land before?" another security man asked.

"No. This is my first time."

The three security men looked at each other, nodding. They spoke softly and rapidly to each other in Hebrew again. The tall, muscular security man turned to Aldo. "We have checked our records, Father. They indicate that this is your second journey here."

"There must be a mistake," Aldo said. "Perhaps it was another priest by this name." He spread his palms in a pious gesture, as he continued. "There must be hundreds, if not thousands of Santinis from Italy who make this same journey."

The tall blond security man looked at his companions and shrugged. "You have a point there, Father," he said. The tall, blond opened the passport and lifted the cover of a portable scanner. He turned to the computer on the desk, typed several key strokes and moved the mouse to activate the scanner.

Aldo felt his face pale, but quickly regained his composure. The man handed the passport back to him. "I am sorry about the inconvenience,

Father, but I am sure you understand that this is a security routine. By the way, you look good in your new beard."

"Yes," Aldo agreed, "my parishioners are actually getting used to the idea." Aldo backed out of the booth and tucked the passport into his pocket. He returned to the line of passengers waiting to board, feeling a tremendous relief from the nerve-wracking ordeal the security men had put him through.

Once the priest left, the tall, blonde man motioned to one of the other security guards. "Check out this travel company and have someone in Tel Aviv watch for anyone disappearing from the tour after getting off the plane. Also have someone follow that priest."

"Right away," the man said, and immediately got onto the computer.

# CHAPTER 33

A ldo knew that he was under suspicion and would be watched closely during and after the flight. He assumed that the businessman seated next to him, absorbed in his newspaper, was really from security. Aldo pulled out a dog-eared Bible and opened it to a passage indicated by a bookmark stuck between the pages. He spent an hour or more of the flight reading, marking the location of certain passages of scripture in neat cursive on the white margin around the psalm, printed in Italian on the bookmark. The 23rd, he noticed.

He knew the agent was photographing his notes and the pages he read, surreptitiously, with a tiny camera on his wristwatch. Let them have fun decoding these, Aldo thought, as he marked portions from The Sermon on the Mount, the baptism of Christ, Jesus throwing the money changers out of the temple, and the Lord's Prayer. He threw in a few more psalms too, even his own Christian father's favorite two lines in the 91st: There shall no evil befall thee, neither shall any plague come nigh thy tent, for He shall give his angels charge over thee, to keep thee in all thy ways.

When he'd had enough of this, Aldo laid the Bible in his lap and leaned back to meditate. When the plane had come to a full stop, the businessman next to him put his newspaper into the seat pocket and got up. While he was occupied at the overhead across the aisle, Aldo put another bookmark of the 23rd Psalm into a small prayer book he took out of his cloak, then put the prayer book in the seat pocket behind the agent's newspaper—for Nadia, the nun a dozen seats behind him. She would pick it up with the newspaper as she went by.

Then Aldo left the Bible on the seat as he got down his own carry-on from the overhead directly above him. The business-man politely allowed him to go first. "Father, you left your Bible," he said.

Aldo turned in the narrow aisle and the man handed it to him. "Thank you so much," he told him. Aldo continued towards the exit ahead of the businessmen, carrying the Bible in plain sight. Once inside the airport, he went directly to baggage claim with the others, then to the street.

Outside, he boarded the tour bus with the rest of the group and took a seat next to a priest named Duval from Marseilles. They conversed awkwardly in English about the sights they would see: The Church of the Holy Sepulchre, the tomb of the Virgin, the Weeping Wall, the Garden of Gethsemane, the Mount of Olives. When they stopped for dinner, Aldo again purposely left the Bible on the bus seat for the Father from Marseilles to pick up with his shopping bag full of god only knew what all.

Aldo quickly moved down the aisle with several other priests and got off the bus ahead of his seat partner. When the tourists all dispersed in different directions for dinner, Aldo stayed with his little group of priests. But he noticed two security men following Father Duval from Marseilles, who had indeed picked up Aldo's dog-eared Bible, and was headed in the opposite direction with other tour members down a side street.

Once Aldo's group decided on a restaurant, Aldo excused himself. He explained to the American priest on his right that he was not feeling well and was going on to the hotel. Aldo then went into the bathroom, locked the door, took off his contact lenses, shaved, touched up his clean-shaven chin with make-up from his bag, cleaned up the sink, and changed into jeans, a linen shirt, and sandals. He stuffed the clothing he'd taken off into the carry-on and went out the back door.

At the first hotel on the street, Aldo went inside and found the door to the dumpster down a narrow hallway and dropped his carry-on into it.

# CHAPTER 34

O nce they'd landed, the nun who'd sat behind Aldo watched his
every move. She had gotten down her bag, noted the newspaper
in the seat where the businessman had sat and calmly, deliberately, took
it from the pocket and carried it openly down the aisle. When she got
to the plane exit, a man stopped her and asked to see the newspaper
and everything in her pockets. She gave him the newspaper, fished out
the prayer book Aldo had left for her behind the newspaper and a small
cellophane wrapped biscotti left from lunch.

"Your passport, too," he said and she got that out of her shoulder
bag. The man read the name in the passport, Sister Jude Goldsmith,
and compared it and the signature in the passport with the one in the
prayer book. "Born in Israel, a naturalized citizen of the United States.
Philadelphia, eh?"

Sister Jude nodded. The man seemed confused. "I'll keep the
newspaper, if you don't mind, Sister." She smiled at him and passed on
to a waiting area with the rest of the group.

Later, when they got to the little hotel arranged by the tour agency,
she went to the room assigned to her and took out the bookmark from
the sleeve of her tunic. This line of the psalm was underlined on the
bookmark: He annointeth my head with oil. In the margin Aldo had
written Proverbs 11:14 and Job 24:23. She looked up the passages in a
Bible she pulled out of her bag. The first said: Where no council is, the

people fall, but in the multitude of counselors, there is safety. And in the second it said: Though it be given him to be in safety, whereupon he resteth; yet his eyes are upon their ways.

She understood. She was not to go to the safe house as planned, nor leave the group except during free time. Then she was to go to the oil warehouse when the streets were the busiest. But where Aldo was, she didn't know. Even the tour group was wondering what had happened to the priest from Bologna who'd left his Bible behind on the bus.

The Damascus gate leading into the Old city of Jerusalem was crowded on this Sunday morning. Merchants were hauling their wares toward the Suk area, and throngs of tourists were making their way toward the Wailing Wall and the Suk.

The nun worked her way slowly through the dense crowds and noted any street signs that she recognized. It was as if she had never left the area. Memories of her childhood came flooding in and she recalled her father holding her hand one sunny morning as they walked on the cobblestone road toward the Suk. He had bought her a favorite toy from a vendor there, a large carved camel made of olive-tree wood. Afterwards, they had stopped for Kaine, the juicy cane sugar she liked to suck on.

Twice a month she would accompany him from their west bank village to the Suk area of the Old city in a horse-drawn wagon loaded with boxes of tomatoes that he grew himself at the edge of the village. Little of the city had changed since those days, she thought.

A merchant carrying two large olive oil cans suddenly bumped her from behind and cursed her as he passed. Nadia frowned at him, but he quickly moved on without acknowledging his rudeness.

In the next block Nadia stopped beneath a sign written in both Arabic and English: The General Merchandise Company of East Jerusalem, Ltd., distributors of French and Italian olive oil. She raised the sleeve of her tunic and looked at her watch. It was almost half past eleven, but what did it matter? She had no appointment and was not quite sure how to proceed. Could Aldo be watching their meeting place to make sure no one had followed either of them? For she was expecting him, because he knew from the itinerary given them that this was the only day that activities had not been scheduled.

She continued slowly on past the place, looking back several times. As the sun climbed toward its zenith, lunch hour throngs began to fill the eateries lining the street and Nadia could smell falafel cooking in olive oil, the strong aroma of black Turkish coffee, and the delicate scent of fresh baked pita bread.

She saw two Israeli border guards munching on large sandwiches of pita filled with salad, falafel, and white tahina sauce. Her mouth watered. She could easily down several of them. She was so hungry, and wished she could have a cup of a strong black coffee with her meal.

Nadia walked slowly back toward the olive oil market, searching for Aldo dressed as Father Santini, among the crowd. She had a sinking feeling that he might not come, that she might never see him again. As she neared the store, she saw the merchant who'd bumped into her earlier coming out the door, counting money he'd received for his merchandise. When he recognized her, he shrugged his shoulders and touched the end of his keffiah headgear, still not acknowledging her.

She decided to go inside the market and inquire about the olive oil in storage, awaiting Father Santini's arrival. She walked up the Jerusalem stone steps and entered. The clock's hands on the ancient wall were approaching noon.

Two clerks were busy with customers. She noticed an older man pouring over a ledger, his gray-speckled mustache turned up toward his ears. The owner, she assumed. She saw that he had a scar near his eye, a souvenir of an old skirmish, perhaps.

The merchant raised his head from the ledger, eyeing her. He noticed her white head cover and the beads she was holding in her right hand. She arched her eyebrows and met his curious look. His eyes were watery, and when he began blinking rapidly, she recognized him,

Selim Aboudi, the man with the tic whom she was told to contact in an emergency.

He was an old Fatah man, one of many of Arafat's retired foot soldiers, and now a respected merchant. But under the guise of his thriving olive oil business, Selim was a known smuggler to the underworld crowd. For a steep fee, he would go to the end of the earth to fetch the requested merchandise, as was the case with the olive oil they were to pick up.

But, apparently, Father Santini was not going to show up and Nadia would now have to step into his shoes.

"How can I help you, Sister?" Selim said in greeting. He smiled at her, revealing empty spaces among his remaining yellow teeth.

"I am here to collect an order for Father Santini." She guessed that Selim would recognize her slight mid-eastern accent.

"Ah, yes, of course. But where is Father Santini? Isn't he coming for it?"

"Father Santini is not well today," Nadia said. "He instructed me to come instead. I will pay you in cash, if it's all right with you."

"Yes, of course," Selim said. "But how do I know who you are? I was told to give the merchandise directly to the Father."

The nun reached into her wide pocket, brought out the bookmark and handed it to Selim.

"Yes, of course," he said. "If you could step to the back of the store, one of my helpers will assist you." He pointed to a door at the back. "And please send Father Santini my regards. I hope he feels better."

"I will do that, Mr. Aboudi. Thank you for everything. You are a noble man," Nadia said. She actually wanted to say more to him, but the two customers at the counter were eyeing her inquisitively, so she began to walk toward the back of the store.

She waited for a full minute, watching for the helper to come through the door. When he did, she had to stifle her surprise. It was Aldo, beardless, dressed in jeans.

"There's been a mix-up in your order," he said, his face deadpan.

"If you will come with me, I'll show you a brand you might like better. Back here," he said, holding the door.

"Thank you," she said, and followed him down a dimly lit hall. "In there," he said, opening the door to a storage area and pointing to a bag. "Switch clothes with those in the bag. Then when there is a disturbance on the street, go back through the store and walk leisurely to the Damascus Gate where I'll pick you up in a cab." He handed her a basket. "Take this with you."

Nadia didn't have to look into the shopping basket to know it contained fresh pita and fruit. She could smell them. She hastily got out of her habit and put on the khaki pants, shirt, and work cap. She stuffed the nun attire into the bag and waited in the dark room for any sounds from outside.

Suddenly, there was a loud siren. She departed the store-room with the basket, went back out the hallway door, and through the store. She saw the old merchant Aboudi, but he did not give her so much as a glance. Once on the street, she turned in the opposite direction of the siren towards the Damascus gate and donned the dark sunglasses that had been in the bag with the clothes.

She did not look back at the store, but watched the teeming street closely, trying to catch a glimpse of the right cab. She saw hordes of people going to and from the stores in the market place and eateries, as well as a dozen or more cabs. Finally, when she got to the next cross street, she saw Aldo stopped in the traffic. "Taxi," she called and hurried toward his cab.

# CHAPTER 35

Massoud's team members began arriving at the Admiralty Shipyard in St. Petersburg and were taken to a nearby safe house secured by Gregory Pluchenko. It took a day or more to assemble them, for they had traveled separately. Massoud got there first, then Enrique straight from Brazil on a commercial flight with one stopover, Stockholm. Sammy Hupy and Hans Kruger arrived by train within hours of each other from Moscow. They rested and ate and went over their plans. Finally, Pluchenko came for them and took them by motorboat to a deserted pier almost an hour down the coast where they waited in the cool air. Finally, several hours after sundown, the sub suddenly broke the cold water and surfaced. Massoud gave Pluchenko his final payment and the Russian smiled broadly.

Massoud and his team boarded the vessel, ready for the rendezvous with the fishing boat. They spent the bulk of the long journey beneath the sea sleeping. Then suddenly they became antsy, impatient for some signal from the captain that the long, arduous journey through the dark Atlantic was coming to a close.

As they felt the huge vessel vibrate its way to the surface of the choppy ocean, Sammy Hupy stood near Massoud, talking nervously in a low voice. Enrique looked ashen, like he might be seasick, and Hans Kruger watched with interest as the captain finally lowered the periscope.

The Kilo class submarine surfaced off the tip of Montauk Point in the Block Island Sound at midnight. It's first stop since picking them up down the coast from the Admiralty shipyard at St. Petersburg.

The captain turned to Massoud and offered him his hand. Massoud shook it warmly. "I guess we will say good-bye now. It was my pleasure to bring you and your friends safely to the shores of Long Island. We will break water in a moment or two and you will be on your way. I've spotted the fishing vessel. She is waiting for you."

"You are a kind man, Captain, and an exemplary sailor. I still wonder at this unbelievable piece of technology that you command."

"Yes," the captain said, "This kilo class is considered to be one of the quietest diesel submarines in the world. We've proved it, haven't we?"

"You certainly have. Great job avoiding the American navy."

"Not me, my crew. And, of course, the latest sonar technology—it can detect both submarine and surface ships. Its radar works in periscope and surface modes."

Suddenly the vibration stopped and the captain lifted the telephone at his command post. "Open the hatch." He listened briefly and a smile appeared on his thin lips. He turned to Massoud. "Ready?"

Massoud looked at his team. Each member carried a waterproof backpack containing changes of clothing and other necessities. They wore black wool sweaters, blue jeans, and wool caps. He motioned them to follow him.

"Be careful," the captain advised them as Massoud climbed the metal stairs leading to the hatch. A starlit night greeted him as he reached the deck. The wind was howling from the direction of the sound and Massoud strained his eyes in search of the fishing vessel. All of the team members had reached the deck before he saw it. The boat was bobbing in the rough waters and he could hear the engine purring.

Two of the sub's crew threw a line to the fishing vessel. When it was secure, Hans Kruger was the first to sit in the boatswain's chair and be eased toward the fishing boat. One by one, the team members went overboard. Finally, Massoud, who was last to leave, lit on the fishing vessel's deck.

The captain, Nick Carrera, a burly man with a deep voice, greeted them and the vessel's engine came to life. They started moving toward shore and the submarine disappeared under the turbulent waters of Block Island Sound.

"We are going to dock at the Amagansett Pier on Long Island," the fisherman said. "You guys can help me and my crewman unload the night catch. Afterwards, I'll drive you to your destination."

Massoud walked over to him and shook his hand. The captain nodded in the dark and Massoud took a large manila envelope from his backpack and handed it to him. "A token of our appreciation."

The captain accepted it eagerly and stuffed it into his inner coat pocket. "Thank you," he said in his deep voice. Then he shouted to a man standing at the wheel of the vessel. "How you doing up there, Fred?"

Fred shouted above the noise of the engine and the howling wind. "I'm taking her toward Amagansett."

"Okay." The captain turned toward Massoud and his team. "You can go below. It's cramped quarters down there but it's warm. I'll bring you some hot coffee and biscuits."

The captain looked at Sammy Hupy who towered above the rest of the team. "You look like a bunch of commandos. Of course, I wouldn't ask where you came from." He laughed, and his deep voice carried in the wind.

"Yes," Sammy said in a voice nearly as deep. "We work for the army."

"I figure you guys are special, maybe Navy Seals?" the captain asked.

Massoud frowned at him, annoyed because the man had been paid handsomely in advance for this—and keeping his mouth shut was part of it.

"Well, we are part of an exercise that includes Navy Seals," Sammy answered calmly, looking at the captain, though he could not see his face in the dark. The steady vibration of the vessel's engine and the captain's welcome had given everyone a sense of security and comfort.

Hans Kruger and Enrique were the only ones to keep the strict instructions to maintain silence, which Massoud had given them earlier in the bowels of the submarine. "How long do you think it will take us to unload the night's catch?" Massoud asked the captain.

"Let's see. We'll dock at Amagansett in about an hour. That is if the wind doesn't pick up and the waves are manageable. Then it will take us another hour to unload the fish and crate them."

"And then we can go?"

"After the buyers come."

"The buyers?"

"From the local fish market and seafood restaurants."

"That will make it close to dawn. I was hoping to reach the Red Hook Marine Terminal before it gets busy," Massoud said.

"The highway is still manageable at that hour of the morning. Why don't you all get some sleep or at least rest in the cabin located under the wheel house. You won't have this luxury once we start unloading fish."

"A good idea," Massoud agreed and followed him toward the wheelhouse. The captain opened the hatch, went inside ahead of them, and groped in the dark for a kerosene lamp hanging on a hook on the wall. He took out a cigarette lighter and lit the wick.

The space under the deck could accommodate six people comfortably and the passengers put their backpacks on a wall bench. The captain raised the lamp toward a small wooden table fastened to the floor with angle iron and looked for the first time into the faces of his passengers.

He saw the sharp features of Enrique's bronze face and his long black hair, tied at the nape of his neck. He noticed Sammy's slightly slanted eyes and dark complexion and Massoud's fierce-looking stare. The fourth man, Hans Kruger, was a man of light complexion with a thick blond mustache, trimmed military-style. Nick speculated that Massoud was their leader.

"Anyway," he said, "you guys get comfortable down here. In a little while, I'll bring you hot coffee. All I can offer to eat are some English biscuits."

Massoud thanked him again and Nick was off. After he'd closed the hatch behind him, Massoud said, "You guys did well. I'm proud of you. I guess that rough training in the Bekaa Valley paid off. Enrique, of course, did his own training with Amazons, isn't that right?" he asked the Indian.

"That's right," Enrique said, and his English suddenly sounded passable to Massoud.

"By the way I have a special task for you that we will discuss later," Massoud said. He paused, looking at the three. He knew the road ahead would not be easy for them.

"As for the rest of you, I will stay with you and guide you. We have a difficult undertaking before us."

"I overheard your conversation with the captain," Hans Kruger said in his thick German accent, and Massoud wondered again if it would cause them trouble at some point.

"Yes?"

"You mentioned the Red Hook Marine Terminal. It's in Brooklyn, I assume."

"Yes, that's where we are going after we unload the catch," Massoud replied.

"But why the marine terminal?"

"We need to pick up something there on the way to the safe house."

"What?"

Massoud did not explain. Instead he glared at Kruger. "We'll have plenty of time to discuss our mission in detail, later at the safe house. In the meantime, say as little as possible in front of the captain and crewman and, for that matter, at the marine terminal. I'll do all the talking for the group."

"There will be no problem with me, I promise," Kruger said.

Kruger clenched his jaw and Moussad knew that he had insulted him. But as the commander here, his decision could make the difference between the success or failure of their mission. He nodded to Hans then addressed the group.

"I might not have the opportunity to speak to you alone until we reach the safe house. As of this moment, our lives depend on each other. This mission is an important one, and we must not fail nor disappoint our commander, Kamal Ibn-Sultan. Soon, Rashid will join us. Until then, I'm in charge and will make all decisions."

Massoud paused, looking at each man in turn. "That doesn't mean I won't consult with you or seek your advice from time to time." He waved his hand in a conciliatory gesture and smiled at them.

The hatch leading to the deck opened and Captain Nick Carrera appeared with a pot of coffee and bag of biscuits. "Here's a little something for the chill in your bones." He handed everything down to Massoud, including Styrofoam cups tucked under one arm. "You guys are still on your feet. I thought you would have crashed by now," he said as he climbed down the steps.

Sammy poured the coffee and handed each man a cup, including the captain. The captain put down his cup, took out a pack of Marlboros from his pocket, and lit a cigarette. Without saying a word, Nick grabbed his coffee and climbed back up the steps, the cigarette in his mouth, and the still steaming coffee in one hand.

# CHAPTER 36

The windswept piers of the Brooklyn waterfront were just coming to life as the sun broke through clouds at the horizon. But the rough Red Hook Marine Terminal was already busy. Nearby tall tower cranes were unloading large metal containers from several cargo ships and a barge. Three front loaders carried bags of bulk cocoa to a warehouse on wooden skids just taken off a freighter in from West Africa.

The fishing boat captain headed toward the Beard Street warehouses along the Buttermilk Channel fronting Van Brunt Street. He stopped the van momentarily, waiting for direction from Massoud, sitting in the passenger seat.

Massoud pointed toward a rusty structure located at the edge of the Erie Basin. "That's the place, captain."

Nick Carrera nodded and resumed driving toward an old warehouse. Though there didn't appear to be any activity at this early hour, two delivery vans were parked near the warehouse entrance. He drove his own van close to the wall adjoining the pier.

"Sammy," Massoud said, "Go inside and ask for a Mr. Dowed. Tell him you're here to pick up some containers."

Sammy nodded and opened the side door. He raised his coat collar to avert the chill, stepped out, and went inside the building.

The van's engine idled, as they awaited Sammy's return. "Where are you going from here?" Carrera asked.

"A place near Sunset Park," Massoud replied.

Sammy suddenly appeared empty handed in the doorway, accompanied by a stocky gray-haired man whose potbelly hung over worn out jeans.

Massoud got out of the van. "What seems to be the problem?" he asked.

"He claims Mr. Dowed is at home with the flu," Sammy said, pointing to the stocky man.

"What is your name?" Massoud asked the man.

"Dominic Ballucci, warehouse foreman."

"So where is our order?" Massoud asked impatiently. "We ordered two cans."

"This is a wholesale business. We don't sell in small quantities. You'll have to buy those retail."

"This is a special order," Massoud said, ominously.

"Unfortunately, Mr. Dowed did not say anything about a special order," Ballucci said nervously, looking at Massoud.

Massoud turned to the fishing boat captain, who was paying close attention. "Do you have a cellular phone with you, captain?"

Nick Carrera took out a small cellular phone from his jacket pocket and handed it to him. "And do you have Mr. Dowed's home phone number?" Massoud asked Ballucci.

Ballucci paled. "At this hour? It's not possible. Mr. Dowed left instructions not to disturb him at home."

Massoud handed him the phone. "Call him. Tell him his old school pal Saul is here to collect his order."

Though he understood that this was a command, Ballucci looked hesitantly at Massoud. "I could be fired," he protested.

"Do as I say," Massoud said, moving toward the man, threateningly. Ballucci quickly punched in numbers on the phone.

Sunlight tried to emerge through the morning clouds and two

seagulls circled overhead, their cries drowning out Ballucci's voice as he spoke hesitantly into the phone.

"I'm sorry to disturb you, Mr. Dowed, but we have a situation here." Ballucci's face reddened and he moved the phone away from his ear. Massoud could hear Dowed shouting. "Are you out of your fucking mind? I'm sick!"

Massoud tapped Ballucci on the shoulder. "Let me handle this."

Ballucci handed over the phone.

"Calm down, Anthony," Massoud said.

"Who the hell is this?" Dowed wanted to know.

"Don't you recognize my voice, Tony?"

There was silence on the line. Then he roared, "Saul? You son-of-a-bitch. When did you get here? I expected you yesterday."

"Slow transport," Massoud said. "Do you have my order?"

"Of course. And thanks for everything—the generous payment and other things you've arranged. I'll never forget Maui! I wish I could spend some time with you. It's been so long." He paused to blow his nose. "Let me talk to my foreman. He'll get your order."

"You take care of your cold, Tony."

"Call me sometime. We'll get together, shoot the breeze."

Massoud handed the phone to Ballucci, who listened carefully and nodded his head. "Yes, Mr. Dowed, right away." He returned the phone to Massoud and hurried to the warehouse.

"You know the owner of this place?" the captain asked Massoud, curiously, after a long pause.

"A friend from the old neighborhood," Massoud said.

"You're a New Yorker?" the captain asked, watching Ballucci wheel out two large cans of olive oil from the warehouse.

"Here you go," Ballucci said. Massoud opened the back of the van and Ballucci put them inside. Massoud closed the door, got back into the front seat, and Nick Carrera drove toward Sunset Park.

"You can drop us at the corner of 4th Avenue and 38th Street," Massoud said to the captain when they neared the park.

"You guys are a strange bunch," the captain remarked, watching from his rear-view mirror as Hans Kruger and Sammy Hupy removed their wool caps. Then he saw the tall, bronze-faced man next to Hans take out a short tube from his backpack.

When he stopped the van at the corner of 4$^{th}$ Avenue, Massoud bent down to tie his shoelace. The captain felt a sharp sting in his neck, and his vision suddenly blurred. He felt dizzy. The van jerked forward and he slumped over the seat toward Moussad.

Enrique tucked the tube back into his bag and Massoud got out and went around to the driver's seat and pushed the fishing boat captain out of his way. He took the manila envelope out of the captain's pocket then leaned over the seat to Enrique in the back. "So that's how you do it in the jungle?"

Enrique shrugged and closed his backpack.

"It takes quite a set of lungs to blow a poisonous dart into someone's neck," Massoud added, starting the van again.

They were soon at the deserted piers of the Bush Terminal, where Sammy Hupy and Hans Kruger dumped the body of Captain Nick Carrera into the cold waters of Gowanus Bay.

# CHAPTER 37

A dusty jeep moved along the dirt road leading from the kibbutz to a small hanger where two crop dusters were housed.

The pilot, Raphael Solomon, a retired veteran air force pilot who made his living flying crop dusters had just completed loading weed killer into the holding tank of a Cessna.

The business was closed for the day and Solomon had only come in to service the plane for an early job in the morning. When he came around the corner, he saw the Jeep approaching, leaving a trail of dust behind it. He noticed that the driver wore a work cap, like the ones kibbutz tractor drivers wear.

As the jeep came nearer, he saw that the driver was a woman. She wore dark sunglasses and a khaki shirt. Her hair was cut short under the cap. There was a man in the passenger seat.

He didn't recognize either of them and went out to meet them. Agriculture Department Inspectors, he thought. They came often to check the pesticide used for weed control in the fields of the kibbutz, just as they did in all agricultural settlements throughout the land.

The jeep came to a halt and the pair got out. The man went to the back of the jeep and the woman walked briskly toward him, carrying a large handbag. The pilot wondered what her hurry was, but he didn't have time to finish his thought. She quickly took out a Berretta from the bag and aimed it at him.

The pilot looked at her in bewilderment. He remembered that he had a gun under the aircraft's seat, if he could get to it. "What do you want?" he asked in a tense voice.

The man came up behind her carrying what looked like cans of olive oil. Yes, signs on the cans said Montocivo - Extra Virgin Olive Oil, Made in Italy. None of this made any sense, the pilot thought. He suddenly had a foreboding that they were terrorists, bent on a terrible act of mass murder with whatever was in those cans.

The man knew his way around small aircraft, Solomon thought, as he watched the man open the holding tank. Then, to his horror, the man wrapped a white cloth around his face and the woman held a cloth over her mouth, confirming his worst fear. Solomon watched helplessly as the man unscrewed the cap on one of the oil-cans and quickly began pouring its contents into the tank.

"Oil will clog the spray jets," Solomon said in desperation. "It won't mix well with weed killer."

The woman thrust the Berretta to his temple, hurting him. "You talk too much."

After the second can was emptied of its contents, the man picked up the first one and carried them toward the small hanger.

"Move," the woman ordered Solomon, shoving him with the gun toward the hanger where the other plane was parked for repairs.

Solomon weighed his few options carefully. Without warning, he was overcome with emotion and longed for the laughter of his children and the love of his wife. He wanted to live and to see his family again. "I have a wife and two small children," he said.

The woman laughed.

"It's anthrax, isn't it?"

The woman struck him with the gun and he staggered backwards. They were going to kill him no matter what and dump anthrax over the countryside. He made a sudden lunge for the Berretta, but the man came from behind him with a knife. Solomon ducked the blade headed for his throat and a shot rang out. Solomon fell to the dirt, clutching his chest.

"No," Aldo said to Nadia as she raised the gun again. "No sense bringing the neighbors." They pulled the body into the hanger and left it next to the disabled plane.

Aldo Gardini climbed onto the wing of the Cessna and Nadia Tlass followed him. He got into his seat and she opened the passenger door to hers.

Aldo turned to her. "We might not make it back."

"I know."

They were silent as he checked the various gauges.

"The place was supposed to be closed Mondays," she said.

"If we're lucky, no one will miss him for a few hours. Ready?"

She nodded and he started the engine and taxied the Cessna out of the hanger toward the small airstrip. "If I fly low enough, radar won't pick us up. We'll come back for the jeep, hide the body, and disappear."

"How long to Tel Aviv?"

"I calculate about twenty minutes."

He switched the radio to the air traffic controller frequency. "Will see if they notice us."

They listened to the squawky radio as incoming and outgoing pilots of larger aircraft either received clearance or instructions to wait. Aldo revved up the engine then and the Cessna responded, lifting off the ground. Soon they were airborne, over the new growth of wheat in the fields strung astride the main highway east of Tel-Aviv.

Nadia looked down on the kibbutz buildings below, growing smaller. The monotone sound of the engine calmed her and she felt some relief from her anxiety. She and Aldo were on their way to achieving the goal of the mission Rashid had assigned them. So far, they had been able to outsmart their pursuers, after losing them in the old city of Jerusalem that she knew so well.

Would their luck hold? She wondered. She watched the scenery go by, as Aldo made a steady run toward the city.

Solomon knew he was bleeding to death. But if he could just find the strength, he could climb the wing to the cockpit. He got to his knees, holding his chest with one hand. After what seemed an interminable length of time, he crawled to the box of rags the mechanics used and grabbed several and stuffed them in his shirt to stop the blood. Leaning on the box, he got to his feet and held onto the plane. He kicked the box over and painstakingly stepped onto it. Then pulling himself up to grab the wing, he used every reserve of strength to hoist himself further, praying to God to provide the rest. Once on the wing, he lay there, feeling his heart pounding and his lungs filling with whatever blood wasn't coming through the rags. He inched along the wing to the door, rested briefly then heaved himself into the open window. He was head first against the seat, his feet out the window, but in reach of the radio. Please work, he thought, as he turned it on.

"May day, May Day . . ." Solomon was gasping. He felt faint and tried to stay conscious. Suddenly, a loud voice jarred him.

"We read you, loud and clear. Give us your position."

"Cessna duster . . . heading west to Tel Aviv," he said, blood dripping down his chest onto his face.

"Hang on buddy, I can't hear you. Repeat. Repeat!"

"Cessna east of Tel Aviv. Anthrax."

"Gotcha, buddy. Give us a location and we'll send help."

"I love my family," he said. "Tell them."

"I promise," the air controller said. "Hold on buddy, give us your locale."

Solomon couldn't answer. It occurred to him that he'd neglected to fix his son's bike for weeks, though he had promised. If he could have said anything more, it would have been, I'm sorry, Isaac.

# CHAPTER 38

The Cessna flew over the approaches to Tel-Aviv and Nadia saw long lines of rush hour traffic crawling on the coastal highway toward the city below.

"Get ready," Aldo yelled over the noise of the engine. "We're going to make a pass over the city and spray the streets and those lines of vehicles. When I holler, begin spraying!"

"Okay."

He looked at the fuel gauge and saw that the fuel supply was dwindling. He not only had miscalculated the distance but the gauge was obviously faulty.

He piloted the Cessna over the clogged highways and soon the streets of Tel-Aviv came into view. He saw people crowding the sidewalks as they left their offices to join the rush hour traffic. He could even see patrons sitting in outdoor cafes looking up at the plane.

"Get ready," he shouted to Nadia. "Now!"

Nadia activated the spray mechanism and suddenly they saw a white spray following the aircraft, slowly descending onto the streets and congested traffic below.

"We did it!" Nadia suddenly burst into a roar and pounded her chest. "It worked!"

Aldo smiled. Still he was worried. He knew that the authorities had to have surmised that something was wrong, what with a civilian aircraft flying over a major city. Surely, they had identified the number on the Cessna's tail. He turned the plane around, heading back to the hanger where they'd left the jeep.

Two military helicopters came out of the north and were suddenly hovering over the aircraft. He could see the pilots waving to him to land in the field below.

"Keep going," Nadia shouted. She had the Berretta on the seat.

"Prepare to land now!" the air controller ordered over the squawky radio. "Tell them no," Nadia shouted.

"We're getting low on gas," Aldo said.

"Don't waste it, fly into one of those buildings back there."

"We're closer to the hanger!"

"Crop Duster, land now!" they heard again.

"No!" Nadia shouted into the radio.

"This is air control. Land or prepare to be shot down."

Nadia answered by holding the Berretta up to the window. All at once the helicopters backed off and a sudden roar shook the Cessna as a military jet went by above them.

"Hang on, we're going to fly so low those jets won't dare follow," Aldo said. Whether they got out of this or not, at least they had fulfilled their mission. "Hang on," he said to Nadia. "I'm going to make a sharp turn." Aldo Gardini had just finished those words when suddenly power lines appeared out of nowhere. Then it was as though the ground had risen up to meet them. A sudden explosion of fire cut off whatever else he'd planned to say. It quickly spread across a field of wheat in every direction from the crash, sending up smoke that could be seen across the countryside for miles around.

# CHAPTER 39

After an uneventful flight into Cabo San Lucas via Mexico City, Rashid rented a Land Rover and checked into a hotel. The next day, he drove along the Baja California Sur and stopped both in La Paz and Guerrero Negro on his way north. The mountains and valleys were covered with lush grass and cactus plants were in full bloom. The beauty of it all made him wish he were enjoying an ordinary vacation.

When Rashid got to Ensenada, he drove through the port area, looking for a hotel for the night. It had been a long, tiring drive. The air was crisp here in the north and he needed a good run and a hot shower to loosen his aching muscles.

He was on Route 1 to Tijuana and pulled off into the entryway to the sprawling Hotel, Las Rosas an attractive adobe style structure. Rashid parked and went in to register.

From the lobby, Rashid could see a magnificent view of the Pacific to the horizon. And directly below, waves crashed onto rock pilings almost to the rim of the swimming pool, giving an illusion of continuity, as if the pool water extended into the ocean.

His room on the second floor afforded him an unobstructed view of the shoreline and the mountains leading to Baja Sur. He could see the unmistakable peak of the Bufadora, where the ocean rushed through a narrow inlet, creating the effect of a giant geyser. Just like on the Danube, he was reminded of the Cayman Islands and Sandra. He felt such a longing for her that he decided to call her after a run and a workout in the hotel gym. Rashid looked at his watch and sighed.

He went back inside, put on shorts, laced his running shoes, and stretched, then hurried downstairs. When he reached the road, he ran for almost an hour and worked up a good sweat. He liked the feeling of adrenaline rushing through his veins. His legs were regaining their former strength.

On his return to the hotel, he went to the gym, lifted some weights and did a series of sit-ups. Back in his room, he got into the shower and let the hot water relax his muscles. He stood there for a long time before getting out. He wondered how Massoud and his team were doing. By now they should be situated in the safe house and planning their next move. It wouldn't be long before he joined them and took over command of his team. But first, he would see Sandra.

He came out of the bathroom, draped in a thick towel and turned on the TV, surfing the channels for some world news. Once he found a channel in English, he threw the remote on the bed and searched his wallet for Sandra's phone number. He looked at his watch. It was six p.m. in Ensenada, nine p.m. in New York, a good time to call.

The phone rang for a long time. Finally, he heard Sandra on the line and muted the news. Even her voice gave him a tremendous lift.

"Good evening," she said softly.

"Sandy, it's me." He heard her catch her breath. He'd taken her by surprise.

"Ray! Are you in town?"

"No, I was just thinking about you and couldn't resist calling. I've missed you."

She hesitated. "You haven't changed. You disappear out of my life, and suddenly, poof, like magic, you appear again to say you miss me."

"I know, but it's true. I do miss you. Body and soul."

"Are you in the country?"

"I will be soon, and I want to see you. Even if it's only for a brief time."

She sighed. "It's impossible. I'm flying to Montreal in the morning to see some clients, then I am off to Los Angeles to a convention."

He looked out his balcony at the ocean and the waves crashing onto the rocks. "How about after the convention? We could meet."

"Where?"

"How about San Diego?"

"All right."

"Let's say we meet in three days. Is that enough time for you?"

"Yes."

"Good. I'll find a nice place for us. I'll call your cell phone and let you know where."

"Okay."

"I am sorry about the past. I'll try to make it up to you, to us."

"I'd like that."

"I'll be waiting for you."

"Me too. See you soon."

He hung up the phone and a news tag moving across the bottom of the screen caught his eye—Two suspected terrorists die in crash of small plane outside Tel Aviv. He turned up the volume and waited for the story to follow. But he knew even before it came on that the news tag referred to Aldo and Nadia. There was no mention of anthrax, however, and he wondered if they were suppressing that information. Or maybe Aldo and Nadia had failed the mission. Suddenly he felt a chill from the direction of the balcony and realized that he was still wearing his damp towel.

# CHAPTER 40

There was static on the phone line and John Devine strained to hear. "Roger, I can barely hear you. Repeat that, please."

"Evidently the kilo class 636, the one the vice admiral said sunk it's first time out, was seen down the coast from St. Petersburg by locals. Then it disappeared without a trace."

"Interesting. Rashid Al-Sharif disappears off the map, a submarine supposedly not seaworthy turns up working just fine, and then there's that plane crash in Tel Aviv. Did the Israelis say anything about that?"

"Yeah, they're sure the plane was carrying anthrax, but they're not making it public yet."

"Here's something else. This morning the body of a fishing trawler captain from Long Island was found floating near the pier at the Brooklyn waterfront. A coincidence?"

"You're saying there's a connection?"

"Possibly. According to his crewman, the trawler picked up four passengers from a submarine off Montauk Point about four days ago. The passengers helped unload the catch and the captain took them somewhere in his van. The van is still missing."

"Did the crewman get a good look at the passengers?"

"Yes, he says one of them was called Saul and did most of the talking. We should have some artist sketches within the hour. I'll fax them over. Hey, got a call on the hotline, I'll get back to you."

147

"Hello," Devine said to his caller.

"This is Sandra Savino."

"Sandra, you've heard from Al-Sharif?"

"I heard from my friend Ray, who you say is Al-Sharif. He called."

"Where is he?"

"I don't know. We made plans to meet in San Diego in three days."

"Where?"

"I don't know yet."

"This is good news. We've needed a break like this for a long time. Really, Sandra, the man's dangerous."

"The Ray I know is not your Rashid. He's just a typical guy . . . with a woman in every port, I fear."

"I really wish that were the case, Sandra."

There was a silence on the line. "I'll let you know where we're meeting if you promise you won't harm him and that you will make every effort to prove he's not the terrorist you say he is. I feel terrible, betraying him like this."

"I can promise you that if he doesn't resist us, he'll have no problem. An innocent man will cooperate. Please, call me as soon as you know where and when."

"I will."

"Here's my private cell phone number. Call me any time, day or night."

"Okay."

He gave her the number, hung up, and called his surveillance team. "You should have news of a recent call on the Savino line."

"Just got it. Someone named Ray Cohn, calling from Mexico. They made plans to meet in San Diego."

"Send over the transcript."

"Will do."

Next John Devine called Roger back. "Listen to this! Your man has surfaced and is on the move."

# CHAPTER 41

When Rashid got to Tijuana, he dropped the Land Rover at the rental agency and walked the short distance to a restaurant called Consuela's, where a Jeep Cherokee was waiting for him as planned.

The vehicle had California license plates and was registered under the name shown in his American passport, which he carried in his shirt pocket, just in case. The plaza leading to the border crossing check point between San Ysidro and TJ, as the locals called the sprawling border city, was crowded with half a dozen long lines of cars, vans, SUVs, and trucks waiting to get through.

It was hot inside the Jeep and Rashid sat impatiently, listening to a radio station broadcasting from across the border in San Diego. The lines edged slowly toward the border inspection booths, as droves of Mexican vendors and young children approached the vehicles offering their wares: blankets, baskets, pottery, tamales, candies and Chicklets.

A young woman carrying a small baby in her arms stuck her bony hand into his window, begging for money. Rashid fumbled in his pocket, took out the last of his pesos and gave them to her. She thanked him silently with a nod.

The line of vehicles moved again, this time gaining an appreciable distance of a few feet. Rashid felt tension beginning to build and he gripped the steering wheel.

A few minutes later, a merchant poked his face into the Jeep offering him a statue of the Virgin Mary, a white sculpture that imitated marble. Rashid smiled at him and shook his head. The waiting line of vehicles edged a few more feet toward the checkpoint.

Rashid moved the radio dial to another station, but it was more of the same Mexican music, the only music he could get without static. Aldo and Nadia were still on his mind, and Sandra. He wondered whether she would keep her word and meet him in San Diego.

The line of cars in front of his Jeep began moving suddenly and soon he could see the inspection booth and the cameras and surveillance equipment that lined the approach to it. He still had ten vehicles ahead of him.

Marriachi music was playing and it was irritating. He turned off the radio. What on earth had happened in that Cessna anyway? He wondered. The unexpected deaths of his team members made his plans to meet Sandra all the more important. Life is short, just as they say, he thought. Then there was the mission before him and the obligation to Kamal and to his men awaiting his arrival in New York.

Had Massoud followed his every instruction? Had he taken into account all that was necessary for the mission to succeed? He just hoped the team, like Nadia and Aldo, hadn't run into insurmountable problems.

The waiting line of vehicles opened up and he finally faced the border-crossing officer, a woman. Her light green eyes looked at him with curiosity. He noticed her gun, tucked into a canvas holding pouch.

"What are you bringing from Mexico?"

"Nothing, really."

"Your citizenship?"

"U.S."

"What did you do in Mexico?"

"Just visiting Baja," he said in a friendly, calm voice looking straight into her eyes. He was clean-shaven and his hair was his natural color, matching the photo in the passport. His eyes looked green, tinted by the special lenses that he wore.

"You were not born in the US," the woman said, surprising him.

"No, in Israel," he lied. This was the information given in his passport.

"So where were you naturalized?" the woman asked.

"New York City."

She looked at him then consulted the computer screen in her booth. She smiled slightly. "It looks like everything is in order. Do you have any produce with you?"

"No." He felt the tension grip his neck muscles, and the palms of his hands were sweaty.

"More than two bottles of alcohol?"

"No alcohol."

"Have a good day, Sir."

"Thank you, Ma'am," he said.

Rashid drove past the inspection booth and into the United States, on the road leading to the San Diego freeway.

# CHAPTER 42

The grim-faced prime minister paced before the draped window in his office. A strong wind had come in from the Mediterranean and it was causing heavy rain to beat against the pane. He turned toward the Chief of the Mossad sitting next to General Golan. "How was this possible? How could they have penetrated our security?"

Golan looked at the Mossad chief, who nodded. "We have most of the details," Golan said.

The prime minister sat down at his desk and looked at the ceiling as General Golan talked.

"The owner of the Cessna was found dead in an airplane at a hanger a few miles from the crash site. Two empty cans were found there also and the lab identified residues of anthrax in them. We have people out checking the air and fields for any evidence of contamination. But according to an entry made in the log at the hanger shortly before the crash, the Cessna's holding tank was almost full of a concentrated weed killer when the anthrax was put in. We have every reason to think, at least so far, that it killed the anthrax spores."

"Pure luck," the prime minister said, looking at Golan. He couldn't help notice how Golan's grief over losing his daughter had affected the man. Not only his face but his posture and voice. He was a man on the verge of not giving a damn. "And have you identified the two in the Cessna?"

"We're sure the woman was Nadia Tlass from the description given to us by one of the helicopter pilots. The pilot could have been Aldo Gardini. We are sending any remains we can find of the two—and the plane—to the lab."

"This could eliminate a couple of the most wanted terrorists on our list," the Mossad chief added.

"But how did they get into Israel and how did they get the anthrax in?" the prime minister asked.

Golan stood up and walked toward the window, looking out at the storm. "We're not sure. The original contents of the cans, was probably olive oil, but the lab's making certain. We're checking out every distributor in the country of that particular brand, but right now the cans are our only lead. Oh, except for a suspicious priest, that is. This priest flew in last week from Bologna and evaded security once his flight landed. We think he was Aldo Gardini."

"Just make sure there's no more anthrax out there. Put out alerts on every large gathering, all modes of transport, and every other damn thing, and see that there's no more breaches in security!"

"Done," General Golan said.

"Now, what about Rashid Al-Sharif?" the prime minister asked the Mossad chief.

"We are in touch with the Americans. They say he was spotted entering the country from a Mexican border crossing," the Mossad chief answered. "As Kamal Ibn-Sultan's primary lieutenant, he controlled everything done by Nadia Tlass and Aldo Gardini."

"You've told the Americans about this?"

"Yes, they're fully briefed" Golan said. "I spoke to John Devine at the CIA."

There was a knock on the door. "Ben Shamir is here," his secretary said.

"Send him in."

Ben Shamir entered and shook hands all around. He was dressed as though he had just come from the crash site. He was wet from the rain and his shoes and trousers were muddy. "What do you have, Ben?" Golan asked.

"A cab driver left for dead in the old city told us his vehicle was stolen by a passenger carrying two olive oil cans like the ones used for the anthrax. We searched the area where the man was found; it was not far from an oil merchant who turns out to be a known smuggler. Selim Aboudi. At the moment, we're checking on the Italian company that imports this brand."

"This is incredible," the Prime Minister said. "We must get to the source."

"We're working on it," Ben assured him, as he got out a folder from his briefcase. "Also, here is the report from the CIA regarding a sighting of that kilo class 636 submarine we've been trying to find."

# CHAPTER 43

After registering at the hotel and leaving a message for Sandra, Rashid went outside and walked to the edge of the cliff. He leaned against the trunk of a Torrey pine overlooking the magnificent Black's Beach. He felt his cell phone vibrate. "Yes," he said.

"Can you hear me?" Kamal asked.

"I hear you." In fact, his voice sounded close. They were using the hi-tech, state-of-the-art cellular phones controlled by satellite that Kamal had given him.

"It looks like our friends didn't make it."

"So, I heard."

"An associate of ours will be in contact today, watch for him." The line went dead. Rashid tucked the phone back in his windbreaker pocket, puzzled. He looked at his watch. He wondered if Sandra had picked up her messages yet.

Rashid returned his attention to the beach below the cliffs stretching for miles toward Del Mar to the north, La Jolla to the south. He saw a glider soar over the flat plateau, joined by two parachutists who hovered above the cliffs of Black's Beach.

He felt an urge to put on his running gear and walk down the goat path leading to the beach from the golf course behind him. He could run for miles on the hard-packed sand, feeling waves breaking near his feet.

Rashid decided to try Sandra's cell phone again. Just as before, he got the answering machine. He hung up without leaving another message. He had so little time for this and he wished she'd get here. He just had to see her before leaving for New York. Unless of course whoever the "associate" Kamal had said to expect brought new plans. But for now, all he could do was wait. She was probably on the commuter plane from LA.

After a while he became restless and decided to go back to the hotel. Inside, he looked around the tastefully decorated hotel lobby then made reservation for dinner with the concierge in the dining room.

Rashid looked at his watch again. It was almost half past eleven. Sandra had indicated that she would arrive by noon. He walked toward the elevator and then decided to take the stairs up to his room. He ran up the several flights, two at a time.

Back in the room, he tried again. This time she answered. "Sandy? Where are you?"

"I just picked up a rental car."

"Great, I'm in Torrey Pines in La Jolla. At the Hilton above Black's Beach."

"I know the area."

"I'm in Room 322."

"Okay."

Sandra's heart was beating wildly. This wasn't what she was supposed to do. She had not planned to see him again, but she felt she had to. She knew Ray was not the terrorist Devine thought he was. He was just a look-alike who'd been born in Israel and fit some profile. She would call John Devine later, she decided, as she pulled into the parking lot of the hotel.

Entering through the side door, she went directly to his room, taking the stairs to avoid detection. She did not trust the CIA. She was out of breath when she knocked on the door.

Rashid opened it, pulled her inside, and kicked the door shut behind her. He put his arms around her and held her close, his face deeply into her beautiful hair. "Oh, Sandy. It's been so long. I've missed you so much."

She said nothing, but kissed him passionately, with unexpected tears in her eyes. They moved to the bed and he pulled off her clothes, then his own. Oh, how can something so good, be so wrong? She wondered. Then all thoughts ceased, for he was devouring her, taking her with wild abandon. She matched him kiss for kiss, and they moved in a rhythm that only comes from intimacy and familiarity.

Finally spent, they lay quietly holding each other. "How long can you stay?" She asked.

He raised himself to his elbow and caressed her cheek, then smoothed her damp hair from her face. "I have to leave tomorrow, but at least we'll have this evening."

"We'll have a romantic dinner in the room and make love all night. After all, you can sleep tomorrow on the plane," she teased.

Rashid agreed, kissing her softly.

Sandra sat on the side of the bed and looked at him longingly. "I'm sorry, I have a few calls to make for work. Do you mind?"

"No, I'd like to go for a run anyway."

"When you come back, we'll shower together and plan our dinner." She rubbed his curly head mischievously, just barely eluding his grab for her. Though smiling on the outside, inwardly she felt sick. She had just made the most difficult decision of her life.

"You better cancel our dinner reservations, too."

"You made reservations?"

He nodded.

She was overwhelmed suddenly. But she knew she couldn't take the chance that she was wrong about him. God only knew she'd been wrong about men before. But a mistake this time would not just be about her. She had to do this, despite her feelings, despite knowing that he would never forgive her.

Nevertheless, the whole thing was tearing her apart.

Rashid was happy to go for a run. He kissed her and went into the bathroom to rinse off. He put on his running clothes. "How long do you think you'll be?" he asked her.

"About an hour or so. You know, there's a great bike path you can run on."

"No, I'm going down to the beach. Want to come?"

"I wish I could."

He gathered his key-chain and cell phone and put them in his pocket, then grabbed a cap from his bag that he often wore running. It had a Seattle Seahawks logo on it. He kissed her lightly on the forehead. "I can really use a good run."

She smiled and waved. After he closed the door, she sat down on the bed. Her heart was racing madly and her hands were sweaty as she called John Devine's private number. Trembling with emotion, she gave him the information he needed.

When she hung up the phone, the trembling became shudders and spasms of grief. Tears fell and she prayed: Please let him surrender without a fight, please let him live. Somehow, she knew that it wouldn't happen that way. Somehow, she knew he would be gone from her forever. Her tears flowed both for Ray and for herself, for her loss. She knew, too, that she would carry this wound inside her always.

———

Rashid donned his sunglasses as he hurried down the stairs. He went through the lobby, heading for the beach. He crossed the giant golf course that sloped gently toward the cliffs above Black's Beach. Suddenly from behind some bushes, a grounds keeper appeared on a cart full of bedding plants.

"Ibrahim?" Rashid said, startled. "What are you doing here?"

Ibrahim motioned him to come behind the high thick bushes. "Quick, change clothes with me, you're in danger." Rashid knew that Ibrahim's presence alone signaled an emergency. He climbed out of his shorts and put on his old friend's gardening shirt, pants and straw sun hat.

"Your wallet too," Ibrahim said. "Here, new identification and keys to a late model green Toyota pickup with a bunch of gardening tools in the back. It's parked two rows north of the jeep you picked up in Mexico. Drive up 101, obey all traffic rules, and do not call attention to yourself.

"Here," he said and handed him back his cell phone. "You keep it, but I'll take those sunglasses. Someone will call you with further instructions. Don't contact anybody, period, until you hear from Kamal."

"Got it."

"Where were you headed?"

"Down that path to the beach."

Ibrahim put on the Seattle Seahawks cap and walked briskly toward the goat path leading from the high cliff toward the beach. Rashid climbed onto the cart and drove up to an area where similar carts were parked and walked through a gate to the parking lot.

A low tide greeted Ibrahim and the wet sand was packed. It was hot and he took off Rashid's shirt and removed his running shoes, which were too tight. He could feel the sand and the occasional splash from the foamy waves. He left the shoes and shirt behind a cluster of rocks and clutched Rashid's key chain in his hands. He stretched and began to run, just as his old friend would have.

He headed south toward La Jolla where he planned to disappear behind a boulder outcropping and pick up the deep-sea diving equipment he had left there. A light breeze blew in from the direction of the water and when he raised his head, he saw a glider soar over the cliffs.

Ibrahim increased his speed. He was running at a steady six-mile-per-hour pace, he guessed, a speed under Rashid's who was the better athlete. Three parachutists suddenly appeared at the edge of the plateau and their open chutes caught the breeze coming off the ocean. They soared over the beach, casting a shadow over Ibrahim's path.

As he continued running, he saw a team of nude volleyball players ahead, among them several young women. One of them caught his eye. She was lean and tan, and as she raised her hands to hit the ball her breasts collided. He smiled, enjoying the sight.

He felt the sweat building and the blood flowing through his veins. A helicopter flew over the cliffs from the direction of the glider port, casting a larger shadow than the ones the parachutists had made. When Ibrahim looked up, he noticed several ropes tumble from the helicopter's belly, followed by men in camouflage, descending quickly toward the beach.

This was no military exercise, Ibrahim thought, looking around. Four men were running behind him and he noticed they all held weapons.

He clutched the key-chain in his hand and continued running south. Ibrahim looked back again and suddenly noticed a boat speeding up in the waves, moving parallel to the beach. He frowned. He was abreast of the volleyball players and several shouted in victory, as the young, slim woman smashed the ball into her opponent's court.

The four men were gaining on him and fear suddenly gripped Ibrahim's chest. He was not going to escape, he thought. They were too close. Someone had betrayed Rashid, he decided. Could it have been the woman Rashid had met here? But there was no time to warn him now. Ibrahim maneuvered back toward the cliffs, looking desperately for a path back to the plateau. The four men were now moving in a semi-circle, closing in on him.

He stopped, turned, and looked straight at the four. One of them was aiming a Glock at him, ready to shoot. When he looked toward the cliffs, he saw a glint of metal shining in the soft sunlight. Ibrahim pulled out the hand grenade he carried in a belt at his waist. He felt a searing pain in his leg and sank to his knees in the sand. When he looked up, he saw the nude woman serve the volleyball again and uniformed men racing toward him with guns drawn. He pulled the pin on the grenade and waited until the men were several yards away, then threw it on the ground between them.

On the cliff above, Roger lowered the scope of his gun and cursed. He spoke rapidly into a black button attached to his lapel. "Holy Christ," he said, as the huge explosion rocked the very cliff he lay on. "Eric, can you hear me?"

"Yes."

"Are you okay?"

"No, sir. But I believe your long-sought Rashid Al-Sharif is officially dead."

Roger sighed. "The cost was too high." He took out his field glasses and scanned the beach from the cliff's position. He saw one commando on his knees in prayer for the dead and another kicked at the sand viciously in frustration.

"It looks like the bastard used a grenade typical of suicide bombers," Roger told Eric.

"I'm going down. Why don't you join us?" Eric LaGrange said, already descending the steep goat path toward his men.

"On my way," Roger acknowledged. He disassembled his rifle-scope and stored it in the canvas bag, along with the rifle. He slung the bag over his shoulder and began the steep climb down the cliff.

# CHAPTER 44

———

L inda turned on the lamp beside the bed. "Okay, you've been
tossing and turning for hours."

Roger stared up at the ceiling.

"What's troubling you," she asked, stroking his chest.

"I don't know. I just don't think he's dead."

"Who?"

"Rashid Al-Sharif."

"What? You're one of the guys who saw him die!"

"I know. I just don't think it was him."

"You think some tourist blew up?"

"No. The man was no ordinary beach-dude. He was armed with
the explosive that killed him. And he fits our guy's description. That's
the trouble, he could well have been Al-Sharif."

"Well, if he wasn't, then what happened to him?"

"Maybe Sandra Savino set us up. Or maybe she was having an affair
with an operative we just thought was Rashid. Maybe the whole thing
was a ruse to distract us."

"Didn't Sandra ID the body?"

"What body? If we're lucky, we'll find a few pieces. She did identify
his shoes, shirt, and a Seattle Seahawks cap though."

"What about DNA?"

"Fine. But whose do we match it to? No one, and I mean no one we know in the world, has Al-Sharif's DNA or fingerprints. We didn't even know him by that name until lately. He was just known as 'The Waterboy.'

"You're back to your only clue: Sandra."

"Yes, I'm going to talk to Devine in the morning."

"But you're still worrying."

"I'm thinking."

"Now what?"

"If Sandra set us up, of course she would identify the clothing as Rashid's. Maybe it's better just to continue surveillance on her."

"Somehow I don't see her as that type."

"Well, I know I've lost my objectivity."

The next morning Roger showed up at Devine's office before Devine did. "He's not in yet?"

"Not yet," the secretary said.

"Isn't that unusual?"

"Yes, as unusual as seeing you here this early."

"Don't you people ever make coffee in this office?"

"I have some tea."

"No, thanks." Roger got up and paced, then went out to the hallway to the vending machine. It was the worst stuff in the world, but he got a cup anyway, and sat back down to wait.

When Devine came in twenty minutes later, he was in a rush. "Hey, Roger, I didn't know you were scheduled this morning."

"I'm not," Roger said, following him into his office.

Devine motioned him to sit, and he unloaded all the things from his arms onto the desk: a newspaper, a Starbucks sack, his briefcase, and a laptop.

"So, what's up?"

"I have this feeling that we're celebrating over the wrong million pieces of a corpse."

"You think Al-Sharif is alive?"

"Yes."

"Is there some basis for this feeling?"

"Not one darn thing. It's just a hunch. I'm thinking that maybe Sandra Savino set us up. It makes more sense than that he'd actually trust her enough to meet with her now that he knows we're hunting him. Unless she was involved some way."

"That is if your hunch is correct."

"Yeah."

"So, what do you suggest?"

"I want to continue tailing her."

"Okay."

Roger got up, but stood there, stroking his chin.

"Something else?"

"Could you talk to her, you know, take her out to dinner to thank her for her help. After all, she's a beautiful, distinguished scientist who's supposedly helping our side. She won't suspect your motives. She'll just think you want to convince her that he *was* a terrorist, or assume you want to go to bed with her like everyone else."

Devine laughed. "I can ask, but remember she's none too friendly with me. And it won't look too good either."

"You mean to be consorting with the enemy's lover?"

"Exactly."

"Well, I don't see it as a problem unless you want to run for president. And I'm not asking you to consort either."

"I'd have to give it some time. I can't ask her the day after her lover is killed by his own hand because of a trap set by us."

"Right. I guess I'll just stew in my own juice here."

"Well, do it quietly. I say that the man who blew himself up is Rashid Al-Sharif and I don't want the press hearing any rumors to the contrary. Understood?"

"Of course not. If Rashid's not dead, I don't want him knowing that we know. Which is why this should be the lowest profile surveillance ever."

"Good, because in case she's an innocent, I don't want her to feel harassed."

"Gotcha."

"Oh, Roger, one more thing."

"Yeah?"

"Take the damn Starbucks. You've been eyeing it since you got here."

# CHAPTER 45

Rashid followed this route to New York City: 101 through one beach town after another, Del Mar, Solana Beach, Encinitas, then up I-5 past Carlsbad. He debated. The traffic was bogged down with tourists and residential traffic, but still his cell phone didn't ring. He wanted to call Sandra, to tell her that he was sorry he'd had to leave unexpectedly and to miss their evening together. He knew what she must have been thinking.

Frustrated by the heat and the traffic, he got on the 78 near Oceanside, east to I-15, and through the INS stop at Temecula, where border patrol officers were on the lookout for illegal persons from Mexico, heading north. He stayed on I-15 until he passed Las Vegas hours later and eventually, after a long drive he reached Utah. Once there, he dumped off the gardening equipment in an alley in Cedar City and got a motel. He carried the bag Ibrahim had left him, threw it on the bed, and turned on the TV.

Rashid was just getting out of the shower when he thought he heard his own name. He came out of the bathroom, unprepared to see the setting sun glittering on outgoing tide from a section of Black's Beach, cordoned off by yellow crime scene tape and littered with police. He listened with disbelief and outrage to the details of his own life and death. He shut off the TV and collapsed on the bed. The cell phone rang and he answered it. "Yes."

"Your team awaits you."

That was all and the line went dead.

———

East of the Rockies, the freeway left the mountains for an immense prairie of rolling hills and occasional buttes. Then the prairie flattened out, hot, endless, hypnotic, turning at some point into a land of corn-rows that reached to Chicago.

But if the drive and landscape were brutal, so were the thoughts plaguing him. As careful as he usually was, as thorough and precise a strategist he'd always been, he had neglected the crucial. He had fallen for the oldest enemy known to man—a beautiful woman. He had let down his guard, gotten emotionally involved, given in to his passion. The woman he'd loved had charmed him like a fakir with a snake. She had played him and betrayed him as easily as a hooker might rob a john.

He drove relentlessly through Wyoming, Nebraska, Iowa, Illinois, Indiana, Ohio, Pennsylvania, stopping only for gas and naps. He ate whatever food or drink was available at service stations and slept in rest stops.

Finally, in Philadelphia he established a base to recoup and make a plan. He got a motel, showered, shaved and slept for over twelve hours in the first bed he'd seen in days.

Rashid took his mind off Sandra by renewing his commitment to the four-point mission assigned him: to rattle the US again during their memorial service at the site of the fallen towers with both a major anthrax contamination and an assassination. The murder of the Israeli prime minister, who would be attending the ground zero ceremony along with the Palestinian and US presidents, would stop any peace treaty signing between Israel and Palestine at the UN the following day. And it would end all attempts to make Palestine a state, as a Palestinian political group close to the Palestinian president would take credit for both the anthrax and the death of the prime minister.

What's more, the anthrax poisoning would shake the American nation's usual arrogant bravado and cause financial panic in the world stock markets. Additionally, it would add untold quantities of money to Ibn-Sultan's vast network of cells from profits made on blocks of stock in the drug company purchased through legitimate means over the past several years—stock in a company that was about to break the formula for the anthrax antidote and vaccine. The very company Sandra, his betrayer worked for.

Rashid dropped his vehicle off at a safe house near Princeton in New Jersey and caught the Amtrak to Penn Station in New York city. He got a room at a dump of a hotel nearby, and then took a subway into Brooklyn. He called the safe house there from a cafe several blocks away.

"Can we all meet somewhere?" he asked Massoud.

"Yes, here, late tonight," he said excitedly, afraid to mention his friend's name on the phone.

"Also, I need you to do something for me."

"Anything."

"Can we talk alone?"

"When and where?"

"At the Starlight cafe on the corner two blocks south of you—as soon as you can come."

"Ten minutes."

"I'll be waiting."

———

When Massoud got got to the café, Rashid was waiting for him.

Rashid scribbled an address on the back of a photo, pushed it across the table to Massoud, explaining in detail what he wanted.

"Follow this woman?"

"Everywhere."

"Okay." Massoud put the photo in his breast pocket.

"This is just between us."

"Certainly."

"I'll see you about midnight," Rashid said and got up to leave.

That night six men sat around a kitchen table. A dim light over a rusty sink was the only light in the dirty kitchen. Even in that light, Rashid couldn't help notice the peeling wall paint and dark spots in the yellowed linoleum where rotting sub-flooring showed through. The chairs they sat on were rickety and squeaked any time one of them moved even slightly. They talked in low voices.

"Remember, even if only one person dies of anthrax, we will cause significant upheaval throughout the world, just by penetrating the security of such a celebrated occasion as this one. And keep in mind that we're only being innovative about last minute changes here. The rest has basically been set up for a long time. Recently, however, your support cells have been working out details as the plans for the event unfold, preparing for any eventuality. Though it seems we are only a handful of men, we are backed up by many more, who remain quietly in the background. They have been gathering materials, identifications, and legitimate contacts for years." Rashid paused, looking at Massoud.

"Massoud, you will be a Hasidic Jew, complete with skullcap, in the crowd as a rabbi and our eyes and ears. You will be in contact with us all by the electronic equipment we will soon have.

"Enrique, can you blow your darts through something that looks like a pipe or even a real flute?"

"If it's made right and I can practice using it."

"Good. We have several possibilities. We have an expert metal smithy who can solder almost anything. And we have an artist that can make a plastic mold or paper mache' cover for your dart gun that can be painted to look like one of those Peruvian flutes. That might be best. It will be light and easy to carry. Also, you'll be provided with suitable clothing. Maybe, we will put you with the clowns or acrobats which they supposed to have at the ceremony. Perhaps you will wear an air-force band uniform or an orchestra tuxedo. We'll work that out later. But first, we'll get you something that you can start practicing with. Someone will be around tomorrow to discuss options with you."

Enrique nodded.

"Albert, you will make and switch the fireworks with our rockets and get into the ground zero area with your former employee's work truck and ID.

"I'll need one person to go with me."

"Right. That will be you, Hans. Though you aren't to speak if you can help it, you will be the least obvious because they think all terrorists are Mid-Eastern."

The men laughed. "By the same token," he told his black associate Sammy, "you will be able to move about freely too. Here's what else I want you and Hans to do."

# CHAPTER 46

Albert Bourg parked in the lot of one of a series of buildings surrounded by high chain-link fence topped by several feet of barbed wire. There were four one-room buildings, two sheds, three larger storage buildings and a distribution center with ample room between them so that any fire or explosion could be contained at its source. Several trailer trucks were marked with warning signs: **Danger. Explosives.**

*Pyrotechnics and Illuminative Devices* a large sign said on the building Albert entered. Other signs on other structures issued warnings like the ones on the trucks. He knew the manufacturing of fireworks was fiercely competitive, especially with importers who sold ten times the volume of product being made in the States. The few American manufacturers were usually family-run like this one. Almost everything here was done by hand and Albert had worked for the Schmidts' for a number of years, first as an employee, then as an occasional well-paid freelance assistant for large displays.

Pyrotechnics wasn't an occupation one could go to technical school for, and there were no textbooks beyond basic fireworks chemistry. Albert had learned the business from experts in the field, initially in a small operation in Naples, then here when he came to the states. The fireworks that the Karl Schmidt family made were well known for their artistic quality, their safety, and for never failing to go off—and never prematurely.

"Hey, Albert, come on in," Karl Schmidt said. "Good to see you." The two shook hands.

Albert looked over at a sketch of a fireworks display tacked up on the wall, a shaped-burst pattern that would be shot from a rocket. "Perfect, the twin towers. You'll win another Jupiter Award for this."

"And, of course, a must—the flag." Karl Schmidt pointed to a sketch on graph paper that broke the design into squares to guide the carpenter who would build the set piece in transportable sections for nailing at the show site. There, thin wooden slats in an outline of the design would be attached to the set. Then lances connected by a continuous fuse would be secured to the slats. Once ignited, fire would shoot along the fuse, lighting the many lances in seconds.

"It will be exceptionally large," Albert commented.

"Yes, and high so that all can see." Karl Schmidt frowned. "The white is a problem, though. I worry it will show too light and not be seen, or worse, bleed out gray. Anyway, I'm working on that. Ready to go to work?"

"Yes, of course. By the way, I can bring in a helper for the firing crew, if you need one."

"Okay, great, because I want to be in the audience for this one. Shall we get started?" He led Albert over to a diagram. "We'll set up here and fire them in this sequence." He motioned to pictures on the bench. "What do you think of a shell-of-shells lead? Maybe stars around a large five-point?"

"Very nice. I think I'd follow it with the big sprays."

"I envision something similar to begin the finale." He got out a drawing and handed it to Albert. "Tight cluster rockets—many stems forming huge bunches of flowers. No sound, just absolute stillness except for taps playing at the microphone. Then the finale."

"The finale being the towers and flag?"

"Yes, indeed."

"You could end that on tourbillions with a titanium salute. A twenty-one-gun barrage kind of thing."

"Very good, Albert. That will work. Can you assemble them?"

"Certainly. I'll get right on it. How long should the sequence last?"

"Whatever you think, we have plenty of time. The finale alone will be a whopping five and a half minutes."

"Nothing that long since the Bi-centennial."

"That's right."

Albert had been working all morning drawing up plans and it was nearly one o'clock when Karl Schmidt popped his head into the workroom. "Want to get some lunch?"

"Sure."

"How about that diner on Liberty?"

The two grabbed jackets and locked up the shop. The streets were busy with lunch-time crowds from the warehouses and manufacturing firms that comprised that section of Brooklyn. A few panhandlers and drunks were among the throngs of blue-collar workers and neatly dressed office personnel. Albert spotted both Hans and his black friend Sam Hupy in the crowd. Suddenly Hupy came up behind them and bumped Karl. "Hey, mister, look where you're going," Karl said.

"Fuck you," Hupy answered, shoving him. A crowd of men gathered to watch, hoping for a fight. "Hey," Albert said, "Break it up." Hupy pushed through the crowd and disappeared down the street and people moved on.

Albert and Karl entered a 50's-style diner and sat down in a booth with frayed upholstery and a torn oil-cloth table covering. "At least the food is good," Karl said, fingering a hole in the cloth. Albert smiled. A large woman took their order of sandwiches and coffee. But when they went to pay, Albert felt his pocket. "Oh, shit. My wallet's gone," he said.

"So is mine," Karl said. He stood up to check the floor. "There must have been a pickpocket in that crowd."

"Damn," Albert said.

"Donna," Karl said to the waitress going by with a tray of dirty dishes. "Can I run a tab?"

"Sure, hon."

"You'd better cancel your credit cards," Albert told him.

"As soon as we get back."

———

Later that afternoon, after Sammy Hupy had photographed and duplicated Karl Schmidt's ID and state-licensed fireworks technician card, he put Albert's wallet in his metal lunch bucket and Karl Schmidt's wallet in his back pocket. He walked with Hans Kruger to the subway. "Now, watch how a real pickpocket works," he teased Hans. Sure enough, before they'd got off the subway, Karl Schmidt's wallet, containing the ID and technician card, was gone.

"I'm just as good," Hans said in his broken English as they climbed the stairs to the street.

Several days later, a 22-year old man was caught by department store security using one of Karl Schmidt's credit cards in the lingerie department at Bloomingdale's. The man still had Karl's wallet and a police officer returned it, his ID, technician card, voter registration, and a picture of his wife. The thief had already spent the thirty or so bucks that Karl thought he'd had in the wallet.

"But the perp denied stealing yours," the policeman told Albert.

"Maybe it will turn up too," Karl told him after the policeman had gone.

"Oh, well, I only had ten dollars in mine. And no credit cards."

"So, you still do cash and carry?" Karl asked.

"Yeah, you know me, lousy credit."

# CHAPTER 47

E nrique watched the silversmith work. He wore a metal hat and goggles and welded, measured, heated and sculptured the silver for hours. Enrique watched with the kind of fascination and patience he might use stalking an animal in the jungle.

Days later, after Enrique and the silversmith were both satisfied with the completed product, Massoud drove Enrique and his shiny instrument out towards JFK to a deserted area near the once grand Coney Island to practice shooting at targets.

"Can't you run around with that?" he said of the target. "So, I can get a true feel?"

"You must be joking," Massoud said, moving another several feet from the target.

Actually, Enrique was not. This was not challenging. It was like throwing a rock into a lake when what he needed was to toss a pebble into the center of a cup bobbing in the current at the furthest edge of a fast-flowing river.

# CHAPTER 48

A lbert, wearing all cotton clothing and rubber-soled shoes, rubbed his hands on the grounded copper plate, provided outside the large process building to reduce sparks caused by static electricity. In this building everything was explosion-proof, wiring, switches, heating, thermostats, telephones, air conditioners. Even light bulbs were encased in protective wire covers in case one popped, and the floors in the flash powder areas were grounded.

Along the long walls, shelving held supplies, identified with labels for the different categories: Oxidizers; Fuels; Coloring agents; Binders; Sparks; Hand Tools; Supplies. The latter included rows of Kraft paper, cardboard tubes, string, resins, glues, pastes, fuses, electric squibs, flares, steel pipes, aluminum tubes, and high-density polyethylene mortars.

Albert's mission was great weight on his mind. He needed to design a special carrier shell for the anthrax that would burst around it and release it unharmed. He wanted to launch the carrier shell in a mortar tube, probably of high-density polyethylene, as a steel or aluminum tube would require him to weld it at one end and bury three-quarters of its bulk into the ground-a big nuisance.

Albert began staying evenings after everyone had gone for the day. First the secretary left to catch her train, then the several who worked in distribution and other office people. Finally, the hard-working family members, Karl and his sons, Oscar and Charles, would leave too.

After everyone left, Albert let Hans in to help him. Once he had it all figured out, the two made cylindrical casings shaped like bundt cake pans with a special paper called chipboard. This way they could fill the insert-hollows of each casing with black powder and leave the shells of anthrax undisturbed and packed around it until fired.

They donned respiratory masks, goggles, and rubber gloves and carefully filled the casings with the anthrax. Next, they loaded the black powder into the insert tubes, sealed them, and attached the fuse that would connect them to a lifting charge at the bottom of the carrier shell. They then wrapped each casing, first with cotton string in a complex pattern to create a strong wall, then with damp brown paper that had been soaked with a special paste that when dry would give each break container extra resistance to the explosion.

When they were done wrapping, Albert labeled them carefully: *Ground Zero Special Exhibit*. Then Hans helped take the containers to the warming room where they placed them in their own bunker to dry.

Several days later, Albert checked the dry shells for nicks, cracks, and holes. He substituted another batch of fireworks for test-firing and gave his special batch the other's control number in the batch records. He then put the fire-tested batch back in with those still needing testing.

Albert was caught off guard that afternoon when Karl came in and took one of the anthrax-packed carrier shells from its bunker. "What's going on?" he demanded.

"We have to submit a sample of everything for thermal stability testing before the Department of Transportation will let us transport it."

"I thought that was just for crossing state lines."

"Nope," he said, going to another bunker.

"The DOT tests them?"

"Nope, an independent."

Albert was panicking and just stood there watching Karl wheel the samples out. He knew that to pass, the samples had to withstand a temperature of 167 degrees Fahrenheit for 48 hours without decomposing or igniting. He followed Karl outside. The parking lot was full of employees leaving for lunch. But Karl evidently was going to skip lunch and take the samples directly.

"What's wrong?" Karl teased. "Afraid your sample won't pass muster?"

Albert didn't answer.

"Have faith in your work, Albert. Your pieces have never failed before."

Yeah, he thought, but normally, should a sample fail, the DOT simply forbade its transportation. But in this case, the testers would be dead and his mission compromised. Albert said nothing and lit a cigarette as Karl backed out of the space and drove off.

Albert agonized over the possibilities for the next several days, but dared not confide his dilemma to Hans. Meanwhile, as head of the firing crew, Albert had to go over to the launch area to determine exactly where to set up his station. He tried to forget the testing and concentrate on other things that might go wrong and cause the mission to fail.

For one, the shooting site was supposed to be placed far from any buildings or areas where spectators would be and barriers had already been erected to keep people out of the firing area. All mortars were supposed to be aimed at an angle that would prevent burning shell casings from falling onto viewers, cars or nearby buildings. But Albert needed his special shells fired in exactly their direction, which would take some careful planning. Here Hans would be an enormous help. Hans could fire a blank prior to the real thing to check the direction of flight and the effect of the wind.

Albert also worried that local fire departments would have people on hand at the firing site and Albert didn't want any of them getting in his way.

To Albert's relief, a couple days later, he heard the secretary tell Karl that the laboratory had faxed over their report. All shells had passed and received approval and classification for transporting.

# CHAPTER 49

Rashid took the E train to City Corp, walked east to First, then along FDR drive in view of the UN, then north until he was near Sandra's apartment building. He was in jeans and a shirt and carried a canvas shopping bag. He walked back to Second Avenue, crossed at the light, and sat in a cafe by the window, ordered a sandwich, and studied the various buildings up and down the block across the street.

The next day, he returned, dressed similarly with the same bag, and took another seat at the window in the cafe and ordered a soup and salad. He saw a couple come out of the building across the street and hail a cab. Then a young man emerged with a briefcase and walked to the bus stop.

When a plumbing truck drove up, Rashid put down his fork and watched as the truck double-parked. A workman in blue got out and went inside. Won't work, he thought, and resumed eating. But a few minutes later, a Fed Ex truck pulled out of a delivery zone and another vehicle, a furniture truck, swung around the corner and beat a late model van to the open spot.

Rashid put down some money and left his food. He hurried across the street to where the men were unloading an armoire. They stopped at a door, and one called a number on the outside entry box. When the door was buzzed, the other man opened it and held it with one foot.

"Allow me," Rashid said.

"Thanks, buddy," the man said and Rashid held the door while the two maneuvered the armoire through the door and towards the elevator. Rashid followed behind them, held the elevator door for them and got in with them.

"The last one we delivered this heavy was to a fourth-floor walkup," one of the men told Rashid.

Rashid shook his head sympathetically. They said no more and Rashid got out on the 11th floor, found the stairwell, and walked up six flights to the roof. Once there, he put on the blue workman's overalls he'd carried in his shopping bag. A label sewed to a breast pocket said Midtown Plumbing. He took a tool-box from the bag, folded the bag and put it in on top of some wrenches inside the box. He waited until dark then went across as many adjacent roofs as possible, sometimes climbing down or up several feet to roofs at higher or lower levels. When he got to a ledge where the distance across was too great, he studied the situation below, as much as he could see of it. There were lights on in several apartments on most of the floors of the three buildings across the yard, but Sandra's apartment was dark. There appeared, however, to be a dim light on at ground level in her building or the one next to it. He went back through the building, down to the main floor, and out to the back area.

He was right, there was a light coming from a main floor room in Sandra's building. Just as he thought, it was a laundry room and he could hear washing machines and dryers. He would have to wait for everyone to finish. He sat down on the ground against the wall in the shadows and called Massoud.

"What's going on?" he said when Massoud answered.

"She's out. Someone picked her up in a limo."

"Find out who."

The sound of Beethoven's Pastoral Symphony could be heard from the wall speakers near the corner table where John Devine sat with Sandra Savino at the Italian restaurant on 46th Street and Lexington.

John Devine looked at Sandra and smiled. "I'm glad you could come. I've been looking forward to this."

Sandra nodded.

"It was hard on you to lose your friend, I know that. But I really appreciate what you've done for us. You're the unsung heroine of this unfortunate crisis."

Sandra's mind was on the music. She had a sudden urge to go home to her piano and just play through the night. She looked up at Devine and tried to return his smile. She didn't know what to say and she took a sip of her Merlot.

"At last this crisis is finally over," Devine said. "We succeeded this time, but the danger remains."

She frowned. "What do you mean?"

"I'm referring of course to all the remaining terrorists in the world." He paused, holding her gaze. "By the way, I admire your initiative."

She didn't know whether he referred to her call to him on that fateful day in La Jolla, or her recent work with Mark Lindsey. Since Rashid's death, she had put into motion her long held intention to try to pool efforts with the Harvard team. "Initiative?" she asked.

"Your research with Mark Lindsey. I hear that, together, you've made remarkable progress."

"Yes," she said, "We're working around the clock to develop drugs to counter the effects of things like anthrax. I've hired a new assistant to spearhead the project."

"You have your work cut out for you, there are dozens of species of bacteria that can be used in warfare."

"Yes," she said. "I heard from Mark that there was a recent anthrax scare in Tel Aviv. How was it possible for terrorists to attempt such a daring operation under such tight security?"

"We're not sure." He took a sip of his wine. "But we do know they were part of Rashid Al-Sharif's team. He was their immediate commander."

Sandra tried not to react. "He was there?"

"No, he did not actually participate, but it was no doubt his or Ibn-Sultan's plan."

She thought she might cry and said no more. How had she so misjudged Ray? Sandra shivered and pulled her jacket up around her shoulders. The waiter arrived just then and Sandra let Devine order for her.

Beethoven's Pastoral was coming to the end of the movement and Devine raised his glass to her, as though to salute it. "I hope we can be friends."

She let him tap her glass with his, but remained silent, feeling a thousand miles away. He touched her hand and, for some reason, she did not withdraw it.

———

Finally, Rashid heard someone enter the laundry room. It was a woman and she took clothes out of the last dryer running. She folded everything neatly, loaded it all into a basket, and disappeared into the hall. Soon after, someone, a janitor maybe, turned off the light.

Rashid waited several more minutes before taking out a wrench and a rag from the tool-box. He wrapped the wrench with the cloth and softly tapped the window near its lock. When he'd broken enough glass to open the window, he replaced the wrench and cloth, removed the broken glass carefully, put his tool box on a washing machine barely within reach, and climbed through.

Careful not to run into anyone, Rashid walked up the staircase to Sandra's floor. He was just coming out when he heard a door close. He watched through the glass as a man wheeled luggage to the elevator.

It was Sandra's neighbor, Peter something, who liked to book red-eye flights when traveling.

Once the elevator door closed behind him, Rashid went down the hall and let himself into Sandra's apartment with his key. Surprisingly, her place was messy. He looked into her bedroom, the bed was not made and clothes had been thrown carelessly over her reading chair. Her cell phone, he noticed, was on its base next to her other phone.

In the kitchen he found dishes on the table containing half-eaten food that had been there long enough to dry out. The kitchen sink was full. What was going on? Had she run off somewhere in a hurry?

He called Massoud from his own cell phone. "What have you got?"

"She's having dinner with a Fed."

"What Fed?"

"John Divine, CIA."

"Right this minute?"

"Right this minute."

"Can you get me his cell phone number?"

"Are you crazy?"

"No, get it!"

"Is this a personal thing?"

"Of course not. I'll call you in twenty minutes."

Rashid paced Sandra's apartment, then looked around for a clock. He used the bathroom, stared out the window at the lights across the river, and finally called Massoud again. "Do you have it?"

"No, but I have one for his limo."

"How did you get that?"

"I asked the limo driver if he ever moonlighted and he gave me his card."

"Okay, give it to me." He repeated it after him and wrote it down on note-paper he tore from a pad on the desk. "Call me when they're in the car."

Rashid was so agitated. He finally went back up to the roof and sat against the wall in the dark to think. "Was she seeing this guy? Sleeping with him? Was this the reason she betrayed him? And what could he do about it, anyway?

He couldn't call her or she'd tell her CIA dinner date and he'd have a swat team over there in two minutes. But if he hid in the building and waited, he would not only worry her, but the swat team wouldn't expect him to be already inside. They could trace his cell, but they wouldn't know who or where he was. He would pick the lock on the neighbor's apartment he'd seen leaving with the luggage.

Massoud was right, he was acting crazy, but he couldn't let her get away with trying to kill him. Just then his cell phone rang. He was so startled that he dropped it in his lap. "Yes," he said.

"They're in the limo."

He hung up and debated what to do. He couldn't help it. He had to call.

———

After dinner, Devine insisted on driving her home. A limousine outside waited for them.

"Do you always travel so luxuriously?" she asked.

"Rarely," he said, smiling.

A phone went off and the driver answered it. The driver opened up a glass partition and said, "Sir, a call for Ms. Savino." He handed the phone through to Devine who passed it to Sandra.

"This is Sandra Savino," she said, wondering who could find her in a limo going up Third Avenue with the Deputy Director of the CIA.

"Sandra. How are you?"

"Who is this?" she said, her heart sinking at a voice that sounded all too familiar.

"How could you betray me like that when I loved you?"

She was absolutely stunned and tears ran down her eyes.

"What is it?" Devine said, alarmed.

She held up her hand to him to stop him from talking. "Is it you?" she said into the phone.

"It is. You may be with the Deputy Director, but even he can't protect you from me. Watch your back, Sandy dear."

The phone went dead and Sandra felt faint. Devine, noticing her sudden tears, gently took the phone from her and held her hand in his. He was asking her something, she thought, and he repeated it. But she could hardly hear his question. Despite an amazing, heart pounding terror that told her she was indeed alive, she knew, to the contrary, that she might as well be dead. Suddenly his voice was very loud.

"What's going on?"

"It's him."

"Who?"

"Ray."

"What did he say?"

"He wanted to know why I betrayed him." Sandra began to cry. To think she'd thought Ray had died an innocent man, in the wrong place at the wrong time, because of her.

John Devine was talking to her again, from far away like before, and she couldn't answer. She heard him call for someone to come stay with her.

In the dark, from Sandra's neighbor's window, Rashid watched as the limo pulled up to the curb. A late model sedan followed and parked behind the limo. Soon a man got out of each vehicle, indicating that she'd told the CIA dinner companion who'd called her. But what had he expected?

The Fed from the limo held the car door for Sandra and walked her towards the building entrance. The other man followed. They were soon out of sight, but the Fed from the limo returned to it directly, and it sped off. Rashid knew the other man had been assigned to Sandra and he waited until he heard the elevator and then her apartment door open and close. Would the man be stationed inside or outside her apartment?

Rashid remained at the window, watching for anything out of the ordinary. Soon a van pulled up and parked down the street. That would be a surveillance team. He got undressed and put on the bathrobe and slippers left in the bathroom. Then he made a cradle of some clothes from a drawer in a laundry basket and put his gun into it, then threw towels on top. He opened the door and locked it with the key on the desk, without looking toward Sandra's door twenty or so feet away.

He left the basket in the stairwell, took the gun and went up to the roof again. Rashid crawled along the three-foot high wall and saw men on one of the buildings across the yard. In fact, right next to the one he'd been on earlier that day.

He was sure the men were setting up an observation station. Probably installing a shooter too. He crawled to the staircase and went back down to Sandra's floor. He carefully checked that no one was in the hall, though he could hear the elevator. The man assigned to Sandra was evidently inside her apartment. Of course, Sandra would not like her neighbors to see a sentry beside her door.

Rashid hurried back down the hall with the laundry basket to Sandra's neighbor's door and locked it behind him. He went through the refrigerator and found something to eat. Then he looked through the closets, hoping to find something he could use for a disguise, should he need one. But the man kept only a rack of suits, a topcoat and raincoat. He did have peroxide in the cupboard, however, and a couple of hats.

Finally, Rashid lay down on the couch and tried to sleep. He would let Sandra sweat it out as long as he could before confronting her. He had until Sunday. Then he'd move on to the project at hand.

As soon as Devine let Sandra Savino and Eddy, the man guarding her, off at her apartment, he called Roger and turned up the surveillance already in place to full-bore status. Devine was worried about her and guessed she was in shock. Sandra Savino did not seem like the most stable person in the world to him.

But Rashid Al-Sharif gave him greater pause. Who the hell had blown up in his place? And why had he called, anyway? Had he wanted the world to know he was alive? Was it his way of saying *fuck you*? And how in the world had he gotten the limo number?

Perhaps Sandra had called his home to tell him she'd be late—she had been late—and maybe his housekeeper, not wanting to give out his private number, had given her the one to the limo, not knowing he was already seated at the restaurant. In any case, Al-Sharif had obviously been following Sandra.

When Devine got out of the limo, he asked the driver, "Harry, do you ever give out the limo number?"

"All the time. It's on my business card."

"Can you tell me who you gave it to recently?"

"Not their names."

"Anyone special today?"

"No. A rabbi and a elderly woman, and some guy who approached when I was waiting for you outside your office this morning. He wanted me to run him downtown."

"Okay. If you can describe them, I'll send an artist around in the morning."

"I can try."

Devine went inside and turned on some lights. His housekeeper had already left for the night. He threw down his keys and called Roger again. "Is everything in place?"

"Almost."

"Okay. If there's any unusual activity I want to be notified. Be prepared for anything, and if she leaves the apartment, have someone go with her no matter what. Even when I pull most of you out of there for that thing down at Ground Zero on Sunday."

# CHAPTER 50

The next morning, John Devine took a cab to Sandra Savino's. He didn't try to call her on the building phone. He simply buzzed himself in with an electronic thing he borrowed from someone at the office. He took the elevator to her floor and knocked on her door. There was no answer and he knocked again. "Ms. Savino, are you okay?" he yelled. The door opened and there was Eddy and behind him Sandra Savino, her impeccable makeup from the night before smeared and obvious. She was wearing sweats.

"Oh, hi," she said, letting him in. "I'm so embarrassed. I took a sleeping pill and just woke up. I must look a fright." She pulled back her long hair and twisted it into a knot.

"I don't mean to bother you, but I'm concerned. You were so upset last night."

"Yes, sorry I worried you."

"No problem." He looked around at the disarray. As he recalled, on his last visit, the place was tidy to a fault. "I hope Eddy is good company."

"Yes, but I really prefer to be alone. I can't even think when there's someone with me every moment."

"I wouldn't put you through this if it wasn't justified. Would you feel better with a woman?"

She seemed confused. "No, no, I just need to be alone."

"I tell you what, I brought some electronic devices. If you let me place them around the apartment, Eddy could stay in the hall or down by the elevator."

"Please, it's not like he could come in through a window this high up."

"I know, but I'd feel better."

"Will you be watching me every minute?"

"Nothing like that. We'll only get serious if we hear someone's voice or the sound of the front door."

She nodded.

"Okay, then. I'll get to work. Eddy, do you know anything about these things?"

Eddy shrugged, grinning.

"I'm going to make some coffee." Sandra said and disappeared. Eddy followed after her and John Devine sighed. He could see how annoying it could be to have Eddy silently dogging you from room to room.

Devine placed the several electronic devices he'd picked up earlier: one audio under the base of a lamp, and an audio-video-directly across the room beneath the second from the top shelf of the bookcase, which made it about eye level. He put another audio-video on the window-sill a little low, perhaps. He probably should have sent someone who was skilled at this, but he'd wanted to assess Sandra Savino's situation himself.

He called his office and picked up all his messages. He told his secretary to cancel his lunch plans. "If you need to reach me, call me at home," he said and hung up.

Sandra knocked on the other side of the door to alert him that she was coming in. He opened the door for her.

"Coffee?" she asked. She held a tray with a coffee pot and two cups.

They sat down on either end of the couch and she handed him a cup. Eddy stayed in the kitchen. "Is there anything I can do to make you feel better?" he asked.

"No, but thank you. I'm just a little depressed."

"You're probably feeling pretty vulnerable too."

"Yes."

She was more depressed than afraid though, and Divine didn't know what to say. He took a sip of the coffee, then stood up and put the cup on the desk. She wasn't even the least bit anxious. No, it was more like she had collapsed from the inside out. She didn't even care that he and Eddy were seeing her at her worst. And what beautiful woman— what woman period—wouldn't react to being caught all undone, so to speak? No female he'd ever known.

"I'll be going, but if you need anything, I mean anything, will you call me?"

"Yes, of course. Can you take Eddy with you?"

"No, but as soon as I know the bugs are working, I'll have him go out into the hall."

"By the elevator, please. I'm a private person and . . ."

"Of course," he said and gave her his card.

"John," she said as he went out, "Thank you for your concern."

He paused, waiting for more, but she simply closed the door behind him.

John Devine caught a cab home and called Roger. "I placed some electronics. Let's hope I did it right. They're so upgraded these days. I tried to put one in upside down."

Roger laughed. "You're getting old, John."

"Old and outdated. So, what's going on?"

"Well, I can see some wilted flowers on the bookcase, but no sign of her. And Eddy keeps popping into view, maybe he's pacing."

Devine guessed that she had probably gone back to bed. Hers was a serious funk. "Have Eddy move down by the elevator. He's probably driving her crazy."

"I'm on it."

"No unusual activity in the building or on the street?"

"Nothing."

"Keep me apprised."

# CHAPTER 51

R ashid had timed the visit from the man Sandra knew well enough to let in her apartment. Thirty-eight minutes. He was puzzled. The man hadn't sounded like a lover. He'd called her Ms. Savino. Was he the deputy director John Devine? He certainly looked CIA. He had that clean, cookie-cutter look of someone uncreative, like he'd never blown his hair dry or worn anything Armani in his life.

Rashid stood at the window. It didn't have the river view. Unlike Sandra's corner apartment with windows on three sides—First Avenue towards the water, 55th Street, and the backs of the apartments across the yard—this one had only the street and the backs of the apartments.

He turned from the window and went to the large desk and sat down in front of a computer monitor. There was also a printer, fax machine, scanner, and above, shelves full of computer reference books and software. He went through a stack of mail on the desktop and opened the desk drawers and filing cabinet to his right. He found tax returns and copied down the name of his host and his social security number. Peter Norton. He found several credit cards and put them by the phone. The guy had charge accounts at Bloomingdale's, Saks, Marco Polo Jewelers, and Lexington Avenue Flowers. Peter Norton paid his rent to the Jacoby Property Management and took his suits to Prestige Dry Cleaners.

Rashid went through a file of business cards: an accountant, a law firm, several real estate brokers, one stock brokerage house, an investment banker, a caterer, a life insurance salesman. He put several of these by the phone with the credit cards.

He called Massoud. "Is all in order?" he asked.

"Yes, we are ready."

Rashid knew that meant the men had their escape routes and contacts all in place for Sunday. He and Massoud did not need to be there and would move immediately on to their next mission. This time Massoud would go with him to meet with Kamal.

"Where are you?" Massoud asked. "I went to your hotel."

"I'll explain. First I need to know . . ." He hesitated.

"What is it?"

"Do you trust me?"

"Of course."

"Are you with me?"

"Yes."

"Good, I need your help."

Rashid had a plan in mind. He called the property management office. "This is Peter Norton. Is the party room available this Sunday afternoon?"

"Only for a few hours, because caterers and florists will be setting up late afternoon for a ground zero party that night," said a man who coughed and apologized for being hoarse.

"Put me down for the hours available," Rashid said.

Next Rashid ordered flower arrangements of his own, large ones, to be delivered and set out on the dozen or so tables in the party room on Sunday afternoon by 4:00. As an afterthought, he had flowers for the woman with the Pomeranian added to the order. Mrs. Goldsmith, he remembered. Then he called a party rental store and ordered a dozen more tables, six dozen folding chairs, balloons and lanterns, and paid extra to have it all delivered at exactly 4:00. "Charge that," he said and read off one of Peter Norton's credit cards. Next, he called the caterer and ordered hors d'oeuvres, a buffet supper, and an open bar for a party of fifty-three.

"You will have to pay a premium for the short notice," the party planner explained, "but a crew can come promptly at 4:15 to set it up."

"Perfect."

"I will fax you a copy of the menu and our agreement," the man said and hung up.

When the fax arrived, Rashid faxed it on to Massoud at the safe house with a cover. "When caterers start coming Sunday, lag behind with these papers and I'll buzz you in."

# CHAPTER 52

Eddy had been watching Sandra Savino's place all day from the elevator, and before he turned over the detail, he called Roger.

"Nothing. So far, she's staying close to home. She had some food delivered a few minutes ago."

"What? Pay particular attention to that kind of thing."

"The guy had ID and I walked him to the door. He didn't go in. She opened the door, paid him, and took the bag. Benson followed him and so far, he's delivered to three other places in the neighborhood."

"Okay. Call me back when he locates."

Within the hour, one of the surveillance crew came in with an update and Eric passed it on to Roger. "You know that delivery boy?"

"Yeah."

"He returned to a little Indian food place a few blocks away."

"Good, have someone go in and try out the vindaloo and the pouri, see if it's a front. Leave a couple wires there."

"Let me guess, you want a report on the food, too."

"Of course." He loved Indian food.

# CHAPTER 53

"Just do it as soon as he comes in and don't make a big mess," Albert told Hans.

Hans laughed. "Man, you're a woos."

"I just don't like killing people I know."

"Then go get us some doughnuts."

Albert could hear him chuckling over his squeamishness as he went out the door.

Albert drove around looking for a donut shop and finally parked in front of a mom-and-pop. He went inside but there were no doughnuts. He grabbed a dozen bagels and had to wait for the clerk to finish putting new tape into the cash register before taking his money and giving him change.

When he got back, Karl's panel truck was parked by the back door to the storage area. Hans poked his head out. "Damn, where have you been?"

"It's Sunday. Everything is closed." Albert handed him the bag of bagels and entered behind him.

"He's in the closet," Hans said, taking out a bagel.

After Hans had eaten several, they packed everything neatly into Karl Schmidt's panel truck, including the rockets containing the powder emptied from the weighted oil-cans delivered to the safe house weeks before.

Albert looked nervously at his watch. Though it was still early morning, he and Hans were ready to proceed toward the Battery Park location to prepare for the fireworks launch.

The body in the closet not ten feet away was making him uneasy. He checked his watch again. They were waiting for someone from the Brooklyn cell to come get it. Though no one else was expected, Albert did not want some family member showing up looking for Karl. The phone rang and he picked it up. "Yes."

"Albert, could I talk to my father?"

"Oscar," Albert said. "Your father ran out on an errand. In fact, I was just about to call you. He wanted you to know he'll be delayed joining you at the memorial. And if our helper doesn't show, he might have to help with the firing after all."

"Will you have him call as soon as he gets back?" Oscar asked.

"Of course, and if I go before he does, I'll leave him a message."

Albert hung up and wrote a quick note and placed it near the phone: *Karl. Call Oscar as soon as you come in.* Then he lit a cigarette, something Karl had never allowed inside, and turned the radio on above the workbench to his favorite jazz station.

After they left the safe house in the Sunset Park area of Brooklyn, Massoud drove Enrique to the subway station. Once again, they went over the explicit instructions they'd already rehearsed many times. Enrique would take the subway to Manhattan and continue toward the ground zero area where the huge memorial service would take place on the site of the fallen twin towers early that evening. There he would take the place of one of the musicians in the orchestra pit, a flutist who would be conveniently missing. Already in the proper shoes, pants, white dress shirt, and bow tie, Enrique carried his tuxedo jacket neatly folded over his arm and his instrument inside a much-used black flute case.

After letting Enrique out, Sammy Hupy who was in the back moved up to the passenger seat. The van's old white paint had been removed in the Brooklyn body shop and the new, gray paint made the van look older. The expert painter had added scratches and dirt marks to the van's shell. Its license plates had been crushed and sheared at the body shop and dumped into the cold waters of the Atlantic, near the deserted piers of the Brooklyn waterfront. License plates of New Jersey registry replaced them.

They were entering the dark tunnel leading toward Battery Park in lower Manhattan and Massoud turned to Sammy. "Did you check everything? You have the ammunition clips and the grenades in your bag?"

"Yes, to both."

"What about Hans and Albert?" Massoud asked, looking in the rearview mirror at the traffic.

"Everything is in order. He reports they are on schedule."

Massoud thought of Hans' thick accent. No problem. His accent wouldn't matter anymore. "I'm going to let you off within walking distance," he told Sammy.

"What about you?"

"I'm going to put this in a parking garage uptown. Then I'll take a cab or subway down later. But I'll be in touch."

After two men from the Brooklyn cell showed up in a beat-up Chevy coupe, Hans and Albert left in Karl Schmidt's panel truck. Albert flashed his ID at the security gate at the ceremony site and went toward the area designated for launching the fireworks.

He and Hans got right to work. They had to be sure the launch racks were firmly anchored to prevent their tipping should a shell explode before leaving its mortar prior to launching the anthrax.

Also, Albert had to have the exact sized mortars to launch the shells, because if the diameters were off even slightly, gas from the lift charge would escape and there wouldn't be enough pressure to propel the shells high enough. He calculated that the mortar tubes should lift to at least 1,500 feet before the time-fuse set off the charge to burst the shells packed with anthrax. He and Hans both had to go back and forth to the van for tools several times.

Once they had everything to Albert's satisfaction, they spent several hours monitoring changes in wind direction and velocity. Immediately before the launch, they would check a final time, as the charge had to be directed exactly in order to rain down on the bulk of the crowd. He planned to light the fireworks containing the anthrax himself by hand, with a long flare—and the American flag too, because it was a set piece. He thought he'd do the flag right before the anthrax, sort of as a private joke for his comrades.

The rest of the fireworks, though, would be fired automatically. Each mortar was numbered and listed on a central switchboard connecting all the wires so it could be fired by an electric squib inserted into each shell's fuse. At the flip of a switch, the shells would fire in sequence, synchronized with the musical program. Hans would handle this part. This way, Albert could launch the anthrax at any point in the program, while the unsuspecting were overwhelmed by one of Karl Schmidt's impressive displays.

———

At two o'clock Sunday afternoon, Rashid plugged up Peter Norton's kitchen sink adjacent to the kitchen sink in Sandra's apartment, and turned on the water as high as it would go. At 3:00 he called the emergency number on the property management lease and made arrangements for plumbers to come fix the broken pipes flooding his floor. "It seems to be coming from Ms. Savino's next door," he said. "But we've turned her water off already, so please, could you pump the water out and cap the broken pipe in my place first, apartment 1110? I'll leave the door open."

When he saw the caterers arrive on the street from the window about 4:40, he called Massoud on the cell. By now, the florist van had double-parked nearby.

"Okay," he told Massoud, "mingle in with the group, but wait until they're all in."

Roger was still on the roof when he got the call. "Sandra Savino has a plumbing problem. Acme called to tell her they're on the way to her neighbor's and then to her place."

"Check them out."

"I did. They are a legitimate firm. Also, we got a catering crew of four and two florist delivery men taking in huge flower deals, all legit too. Some party in the building, I was told. Then some other dude showed up, the party planner."

"Okay, keep me posted. Devine wants most of us to move down to the ceremony, but let's stick around a few more minutes."

It was 4:50 when the plumber called on the building phone. Rashid buzzed him in and waited until he heard the elevator open. He dialed Sandra's number and slipped into the hall. He could hear the guard at the elevator and the plumber talking about the ground zero ceremony and the crowds downtown as he let himself into Sandra's apartment, with the key she had given him last year.

Rashid knew Sandra would answer either the phone at her desk in the living room or the one beside her bed. When she did, he hung up and exchanged his cell for his revolver. He had already attached the silencer.

The front of the apartment was empty and the TV was on. He heard her in the bedroom. He scanned the room quickly for wires and removed two audio-video devices. He smashed them with his gun butt just as she entered from the bedroom. He was astonished to see her looking so fragile and pale, and she did not seem surprised to see him. Instead of crying out as he'd expected, she sat down on the sofa. She was not afraid, just sad. Resigned to her fate, perhaps.

"How could you betray me like that?" he asked her.

"How could you? I loved you and didn't believe them when they said you were a terrorist. I thought they were just paranoid because of 9/11. I didn't think it was in you to do this kind of evil until I heard your voice on the phone and found out you were alive."

She had tears in her eyes and they were both silent for a moment.

"You were probably using me the whole time just to get my formula. So, go ahead and kill me because I'd just as soon be dead. You've broken my heart. But before you do, I want to know why you've taken such an unthinkable path."

"Because I love my country and believe in our cause."

"A cause that allows you to kill others who have their own causes? Ordained by a god you think made you superior to everyone else? But what happens when your god of hate changes his mind and turns on you?"

Now tears ran down her cheek, but she said nothing more. He hadn't expected this and he stared at her and slowly lifted his revolver. She looked directly at him and he put the gun back into his pocket. "I am sorry, I really am," he said and turned toward the door. He looked out the small glass in the entry and saw Massoud coming down the hall. He opened the door to him and Massoud looked as sad as Sandra.

"What is it?" Rashid asked him. He felt the knife his friend held before it left his hand. "But why?" he asked Massoud as he slid down alongside Sandra's open door.

Roger saw a figure in the window on the scope and it wasn't Sandra Savino. Simultaneously, Eric was on the walkie-talkie. "We lost our video, but your guy is definitely inside. You better get him while they're still talking."

"We can't get a bead on him, but I see her on the couch. Send in the team."

"Done."

"I'll leave Benson here and come over. By the way," he added, scrambling across the roof, "there's smoke coming from a first-floor window."

"What do you know," Eric answered. "Here comes a fire truck."

Roger could hear it as he ran down the stairwell. When he got to the bottom, he ran across the yard, smashed the glass on the door and headed up the hallway to Sandra's stairwell. People were running down the hall and fireman were coming in the door. He could smell the smoke. When he got to Sandra's floor, Johnson from the p.m. shift lay dead outside the elevator.

Roger ran down the hallway, but Eric and one of the swat team—and Linda were already at Sandra's door. They were looking down at something and when he got closer, he saw Sandra Savino sitting against the wall in shock, holding Rashid Al-Sharif's head to her breast. Al-Sharif was dead.

This wasn't the scene he'd envisioned at all and Roger looked over at Linda and frowned to indicate how much he disliked her this close to trouble. She understood his message and shrugged.

"What happened?" he asked Eric.

"We don't know. Evidently, whoever got Johnson got him. We also found a dead fireman, but not in his uniform."

Roger got down beside the distraught woman. "Ms. Savino, are you okay?"

She nodded.

"Did you see who did this?"

She shook her head no.

"Did Rashid say anything before he…?"

Sandra Savino started crying and ignored him.

"Ms. Savino, this might be the most important thing you've ever done in your life. If he said anything, anything at all, please tell us!"

"Nothing," she said, wiping her tears.

"You're positive?"

She nodded.

The man standing next to Linda handed him a bag. "Let's go," Roger said to Linda. "Eric, you coming?" The three ran down the stairs, through the lobby of the building, and got into a car parked across the street from the surveillance van.

"The 35th Precinct helicopter port," Eric told the driver as he closed the door on the passenger side. The driver pulled away from the curb and Eric got on the radio. "We need a copter to get into ground zero ASAP. We're on our way." He turned to Roger and Linda in the back. "We'll never get there driving."

Roger went through the contents of the bag: a gun, a cell phone, a wallet containing twelve hundred dollars, a New Jersey driver's license issued to Vito Martino with Al-Sharif's picture on it, what looked like a confirmation number for an electronic airline ticket, and a name and phone number scribbled on a torn piece of note paper.

"Ali Bourigiba," he read and dialed a number. "Parker, drop everything and run down this phone number: 548-9065. If we're lucky, it's in the (212) calling area. Locate the address and send someone over there immediately. Also check out an Ali Bourigiba. B-o-u-r-i-g-i-b-a. I'm sending over a Glock and cell phone for tracing as well. Put everyone on this and get back to me right away on anything." He hung up and looked at Linda. "You were in the detail van?"

"Yes, and I heard everything they said. It was spooky. For a moment I even felt sorry for the man."

"You felt sorry for a terrorist?"

"Yeah, briefly. Obviously, the guy loved her."

"Yeah, obsessed enough that he risked everything to see her though he had to have known we were watching the building. And whoever killed him had to think it was worth the risk to do it there too."

"Well, they had enough distractions going," Eric said. "Al-Sharif must have thought his killer was watching his back."

Linda frowned. "So, you think the killer saw Al-Sharif as a sudden liability to something they have planned?"

"Yeah, to something going on today."

"But I don't get it. Why aren't they already down at the ceremony if something's going on?"

"For the same reason they weren't in those planes going through the trade towers. These guys leave the dying to others." His cell phone buzzed and Roger answered and listened. "Good work, send someone over there."

"What's the news?" Eric asked.

"Al Bourg, pyrotechnic expert," he told him, dialing another number.

"Fireworks!" Linda said.

Roger's party answered. "John," he said, "Shut down the ceremonies before the president gets there and confiscate all the fireworks. We have good reason to think they'll set off explosives. No, tell him there's definitely a real threat. Double the watch on all three! We're headed down by copter. Could you alert the cops to let us through?" Roger hung up.

"What did he say?" Linda asked.

"They're headed for the fireworks now, but it's too late to stop the president from leaving. He's already touring one of the exhibits in a building on the grounds with the Israeli prime minister and the Palestinian president. We'll have to try to evacuate them by helicopter. The ceremony is scheduled to begin in less than an hour."

The traffic was heavy and within blocks of Battery Park it had come to a complete standstill. At the ground zero site, a place to land had already been opened and police stood nearby. "Linda . . ." Roger began as they touched down.

"No. Don't even suggest it!"

He sighed. "Then be damn careful." The three got out of the copter and ran across the ground. "Which way to the ceremony site?" Roger asked a policeman.

"Follow me." The crowds were heavy and the policeman raised his stick and had to holler several times to get the crowds to part. "Emergency, make way!" he yelled. When they got to the police barricades, other policemen joined them.

The President walked briskly from the exhibit building toward the area where they would break ground for the memorial that would be built on what was now a sacred national site. There was a huge crowd gathered in stands erected for the ceremonies.

As he proceeded toward the platform bearing the Presidential Seal in front of the podium, he noticed the circle of secret service men surrounding him and the dignitaries behind him tighten.

One of the secret service men listened intently to a message being relayed through an ear-plug, attached to a wire leading to the inner pocket of his suit jacket. The man looked abruptly at the skies above where he saw a police helicopter getting ready to land. He hurried to catch up with the president's entourage moving toward the platform, as policemen held back the crowd.

"Mr. President," the secret service man said quietly, "We believe it imperative that we cancel the ceremonies. We need to evacuate you, as well as the Israeli Prime minister and the Palestinian president, immediately."

The president turned toward the man, his blue eyes surveying him with curiosity. Then he looked up at a helicopter bearing the presidential seal, approaching from the west.

"What seems to be the problem?" the President inquired.

"We're expecting an incident," the man replied.

"An incident?"

"We think there's a terrorist plot in progress."

The president's face tensed and his eyes followed the path of the helicopter's flight "This isn't something we can just cancel. This ceremony is all about not being afraid of terrorists. That's why we're here today. And for the world, it's about peace in the Middle East."

"I know, sir, but you and your guests are in danger."

"I'll talk it over with them. But I'm trusting that you all can handle this."

The secret serviceman spoke softly, but firmly. "Yes, sir. But with all due respect, sir, could you either stay here behind the wall or move to that area behind the glass? Now!"

The president smiled at him and nodded. "We'll stay behind the wall until the music starts." He then turned toward his guests, waiting behind him. "Gentlemen, I have grave news. My advisers say we're in danger. They say we should leave and forgo the ceremony."

"And what do you say?" the Palestinian president asked.

"I say we stay and see this through. Not give in to fear."

"I agree," the Israeli Prime minister answered.

Then, he added. "it's essential that we do not leave," the Israeli Prime Minister confirmed.

The President looked from one to the other and then pointed toward the stand. "Of course, that bullet proof glass will help."

The three heads of state laughed.

———

Albert looked at his watch then rechecked his and Hans' equipment carefully. They would put on the gloves and coveralls before the firing, the masks immediately after lighting the fuses. Going out, they would just look like part of the emergency crews. That is if there was anyone around to care once bodies started dropping.

Now came the wait and Albert smoked impatiently over by the fence. There was this air of excitement all around and the streets in the area were like tributaries to a sea of people. Many of them, if he and Hans had done their job right, would not be going home.

Suddenly Albert caught sight of a suit watching him. He threw down the cigarette and stepped on it without taking his eyes off the man who looked suspiciously like a federal agent. Albert walked easily over to Hans. "Don't turn to look but a Fed is behind you. Let me do all the talking. You have your gun handy?"

Hans nodded.

"If it looks like trouble, shoot him."

"Hello," the man said.

Albert noticed other men in suits about thirty or so yards away, coming through the crowds towards them too and didn't answer. He would have to fire the anthrax before they got much closer.

"Could I see your ID?" the man said.

"Of course," Albert said and stepped closer. "Hans, our papers, please."

Hans reached in his breast pocket and pulled out his gun, but before he could fire, shots rang out from a direction behind Albert and Hans fell to the ground.

Albert debated. He had his cigarette lighter in his pocket. Could he light the fuse to the anthrax mortar several feet away quick enough? He was aware of a shooter behind him, as well as the men coming towards him.

What the hell, he decided, he wasn't that dedicated. Besides, they couldn't link him to Hans or the anthrax. For all they knew, for all Karl's sons knew, Hans had put together the fireworks.

The orchestra members had assembled and were warming up. The crowds quieted as the conductor moved into position. The music began and the president and his guests moved in procession towards the platform set up for the ceremony.

They were playing "America the Beautiful" and Ben, on hand as part of the Israeli security, found it particularly moving. The crowds sang reverently as did the President of the United State. His own Prime Minister seemed touched too, so did the newly elected Palestinian President.

Ben turned his attention to the orchestra, and watched curiously as a bronze-faced man with sharp features lifted a flute to his mouth. But there was something unprofessional about the movement and, suddenly, Ben understood. He shot toward the man, putting himself between him and the procession of dignitaries. It all happened fast and Ben immediately felt a sharp sting and dizziness. He heard a mass intake of breath from onlookers, and a gun fired behind him. The flute player fell to the ground silently, not far from where he himself lay injured.

———

Secret Service men fairly shoved the three heads of state to the stand behind the protective glass, seated them, and enveloped them on all sides. The President turned to his guests. "Are we still in agreement?"

The two nodded yes.

Meanwhile other security people rushed to remove the bodies and calm those in the immediate vicinity who'd witnessed the unfortunate event. People were beginning to panic and head for the exits. Immediately a voice came over the loud speaker and ordered everyone to remain where they stood. Surprisingly, everyone did.

Then John Devine stepped up to the microphone. "Ladies and Gentlemen," he said. "We've come here today to honor the people who died here not so long ago. We can all panic or we can all sit still and let the experts here do their jobs. We will not find any terrorists today if we have a stampede out of here. How about it? If you're with us, sit down. But if you wish to leave, remain standing and there will be ushers to lead you out."

At that people sat back down and the orchestra started up with "America the Beautiful" again and people began singing.

A hundred or so people filed out, but the bulk of the crowd stayed put. And some of those choosing to leave changed their minds and returned to the stands.

When the music stopped, the President stood to speak, tapped the microphone, and the crowd quieted. "Ladies, Gentlemen, and esteemed guests from Israel and Palestine, we have had a tragic incident here today and I thank you all for remaining in spite of it."

He looked down at a note on the podium, then up at the crowd. "One of our guests, Ben Shamir, Commander of the Israeli Mossad

Alpha team, has given his life in service to his country, in service to our country, and to our mutual goal of peace in the Middle East. Let us bow our heads in silent prayer for Ben Shamir and for the peace he envisioned and died for."

Roger could have heard a pin drop as he surveyed the silent crowd of thousands paying their respects. Linda, beside him, had tears running down her cheeks and her eyes were closed. The orchestra started playing "Amazing Grace" and Roger took her hand and squeezed it.

When the music ended, the President looked down at the podium again. "It says here that for security reasons, we will not see the scheduled fireworks this evening. But substitutes are on the way." He paused and held up the paper. "I don't know where they're coming from, but this note says to expect a lot of Mickey Mouse and Daffy Duck stuff."

The crowd laughed. "Now Ladies and Gentlemen, please welcome our distinguished guests from Israel and Palestine who have come to celebrate with us, to pray with us, to sing with us, and even to cry with us, this night, as we honor those people who died in the terrorist attack on this very site not very long ago."

At this the crowd clapped, hooted, and whistled.

The ceremony had officially begun.

# EPILOGUE

Roger and Linda were at an Indian restaurant in the East Village and Roger poured wine into Linda's glass.

"So, anyway, *The New York Times* says the fireworks were a bust. Listen to this: 'We will never know if the specially designed fireworks—and pyrotechnic aesthetes in the trade—that we all looked forward to were worth all the fuss made over them the past few weeks. The substitutes, everyone agrees, were laughable." Roger looked up from the paper. "Damn critics. It's always bitch, bitch, bitch."

Linda didn't comment.

"I know what you're thinking: pretty philosophical commentary, right? But then what do you expect from a humble man from Idaho?"

Linda smiled.

"Other than that news, Albert Bourg says he was not involved in any anthrax plot and whoever killed Rashid Al-Sharif has vanished." Linda remained silent and Roger frowned at her. "Why so quiet?"

Linda sighed, pushed away her untouched food, and took a sip of her wine. "I've had enough. To see Ben die in front of me and you shoot his killer was too much. I can't do this anymore."

Roger took her hand. "Sweetheart, as much as it pleases me to hear you say this, I have to be honest. We've all been through this. Don't count on not changing your mind."

"Nope, I'm through."

"Take some time off. Do some soul searching."

"I don't have to. I've made up my mind. I'm quitting."

Roger ignored her comment.

"Did you hear me?"

"Yes, you're quitting." He looked at her tenderly. "Let's get out of here."

Roger put money down on the table and helped her with her jacket. Once on the street, he got out his cell phone. "We're ready for that cab now," he said and hung up.

Linda looked at him, puzzled. "We can walk, we're only a few blocks away."

"Actually, we have 1,932 miles to go."

"Where?"

"To find the tastiest steelhead you will ever eat."

"You're kidding!"

"I'm not kidding."

"What will John Devine say?"

"Ask him." He paused and looked down the street behind them. "Here's our ride," he said, watching a limo coming towards them.

"What the heck?" she said as the limo pulled up to the curb beside them.

The window opened and John Devine stuck his head out. "You called for a cab?"

"Yes. We did," Roger said.

The door to the limo opened. "Where to?" Devine asked.

"Henry's Fork of the Snake," Roger answered, ushering Linda into the vehicle.

"Good evening, Linda," Devine said, opening the glass partition between them and the front. "Harry," Devine said to the driver, "La Guardia, please. These folks are going fishing."

Printed in the United States
By Bookmasters